Legends from Fairyland

Prince Glee & Princess Trill

Legends from
FAIRY LAND
NARRATING THE HISTORY OF
PRINCE GLEE & PRINCESS TRILL,
THE CRUEL PERSECUTIONS & CONDIGN
PUNISHMENT OF AUNT SPITE, AND
THE ADVENTURES OF THE GREAT
TUFLONGBO & THE STORY OF THE
BLACKCAP IN THE GIANT'S WELL
BY HOLME LEE
WITH ILLUSTRATIONS BY
REGINALD L. KNOWLES
& HORACE J. KNOWLES
& AN INTRODUCTION BY
EFFIE H FREEMANTLE

CRESCENT BOOKS
NEW YORK

ARTISTS' DEDICATION

To Our
MOTHER
We Dedicate this
Our Joint Attempt in
the Illustration &
Decoration of
a Book
R·L·K ♥ H·J·K

May 1907

CONTENTS

CONTENTS

List of Illvstrations

The Full Pages

The Headpieces

The Initial Letters

The Tail-pieces

The Marginals

b

LEGENDS FROM FAIRY-LAND

INTRODUCTION

IN the labyrinth of the far-off childhood's days these *Legends from Fairy Land* were to me the history of a very real Country. In every flower and leaf, with childhood's eyes (so much more far-seeing than our grown-up ones) I could detect the shadows of the Elves and Fairies that stared in amazement at the imprisonment of poor little Idle by the Creeping Plant. I can remember, when having been unusually lazy and careless, passing any stray tendrils of Ivy or Virginia Creeper with cold tremors of fear, lest the wicked Fairy should be lurking in their midst.

In my little white bed at night I think I must have caught the fleeting rays from the moon and stars, and even now I feel almost sure that " Old Woman " is weaving the dresses that I wove for the Fairies in my dreams.

Cbild=bood's Fairy Land and

I think that in every little child's heart there is a Fairy Land, and the little children reading this book will recognise a friend in "Mannikin Hope." How often has he not helped us all when life has seemed very dreary, and grown-up people did not know nor understand the ache in the baby heart! Has he not often whispered, when we have washed our hands and faces with extra care, and mother has not noticed how we have tried to help, " Be comforted, for though she does not notice now the Fairies will whisper it to her when she is asleep "? and when lessons were hard, and the world was all too lonely, did he not take us by the hand and lead us upward to the Golden Light, so that we had strength to battle and win the prizes that we laid so gladly at mother's feet?

The remembrance of "little Maid Brisk" made me become very busy; although re-membering how very easy it is to waste time and be lazy, my heart bled, and still bleeds, for poor little Idle and her terrible punishment. It was justice, true enough, but I think mercy is the best punishment for us all.

Oh, little children, keep your Fairy Land through all the years to come. There is a grown-up Fairy Land too, you know, if you can only keep to the path that leads there, and which your little feet now tread so easily. We all of us alike meet many Aunt Spites, who will show us gilded ways — but they lead only to the Country beyond Sheneland, where the sun never shines. But when on the upward way you, any of you, meet "Love of the Bleeding Heart," take her and clasp her to you, however footsore and weary you may be—press her tightly to your heart—

A Grown-up Fairy Land.

cherish her and keep her warm—and the burdens will lighten, and the shadows grow less, until at last you reach the sunlit summit of the Hill.

The Meaning of Happiness.

Be brave, and truthful, and generous—not like wicked Clutch in the " Enclosed Garden," who said " It is all my own," and then grew grey and cold in her loneliness. Lift up your eyes to the Light, and to you, little Princess, there will come a Fairy Prince, and to you, little Prince, a Fairy Princess ; and if your palaces are not of earthly gold, or your crowns of diamonds, you must remember that they will be of the rays of the sun, and the dewdrops,—just as they are in this Fairy tale,—the meaning of which spells " Happiness."

When in the full morning you hear the lark burst into song as she soars heavenward, you may be sure it is the soul of Princess Trill calling to her lover ; and at night, if you are not asleep, and you listen very hard, you will hear the voice of a nightingale, and that will be Prince

Glee answering her message. Wake up when the dew is on the flowers, and you will hear the lily-bells ringing in honour of their marriage. Look out of your window, and I feel sure you will see brown, white, and speckled butterflies preening their wings in the sunlight in order to look gay when they are harnessed to the wedding coaches. Of course you will only see this in summer, for that is the time of all the Fairy weddings. You will see, too, the bees so busy getting honey for the wedding feast; and the roses and jasmine, stocks and gilliflowers, will have their petals tightly folded, jealously guarding the dewdrops in their hearts so that the guests may not be parched with thirst.

If ever you meet anyone as wise as the great Tuflongbo, listen to his teaching; and if ever you see a little Idle thirsting in the sun, do as he and Prince Glee did —give her, to the best of your power, some Fruit of the Aplepivi.

Dear little children, be pure as the lilies, sweet as the rose, gentle as the butterflies; and, above all, soar with the lark,—then truly your path through Shadowland and Sheneland will lead you into Fairy Land indeed.

EFFIE H. FREEMANTLE.

LEGENDS FROM
FAIRY LAND

"HERE IS THE BOOK"

MANNIKIN HOPE

HE CAN CHEER THE FAINTEST &
WEAKEST ON THE WEARY ROAD

LITTLE IDLE, & the WICKED FAIRY of the CREEPING PLANT with MANY TENDRILS

ONCE upon a time in Sheneland beyond the Moon, where the Fairies
reign, there lived a Little Old Woman
whose house was nothing but the hollow
trunk of a great Ash-Tree. Old Woman
was very poor, and got her living by
spinning the gossamer the Fairies wore
when they went to Elfin Court. This gossamer was finer than any spider's web, and
all over it were sprents of dew, more bright
than diamonds, and silver stripes shot
through it aslant that were caught and
woven in when the stars were shining.

I

Old Woman had a little Maid to help her, whose name was Idle; it was her task to gather the rays as they fell, and carry them to Old Woman's wheel. Idle was fat and white, but she had no colour in her cheeks; and the Fairies did not like her for their playfellow at all, because she was so slow, so *very* slow. If they cried, " Run, Idle, run! the stars are going out, and you have not gathered rays enough yet to make Trip and Try-for-it a coat apiece!" there she would stand, with one finger in her mouth, until the rays were drawn up out of her reach, and then she had to go home with only one or two, and sometimes none at all.

When that happened, Old Woman very properly gave her no supper, and whipped her before she put her to bed. Idle did not like that, and promised every time that she would do better in future; but the next night when she was sent out to gather the silver stripes, she would sit down and go to sleep, until some

SHE·WOULD·SLEEP·UN-
TIL·SOME·GOOD·FAIRY·
TWITCHED·HER·HAIR

good Fairy twitched her hair, or tickled her nose, when she would lift herself up, yawning, and creep along the ground too slowly to catch any rays except those that had got tangled in among the bushes and prickly plants, and could not get away fast enough; and she even lost *them* sometimes for stopping to wonder whether she should scratch her hands in pulling them out; and while she was thinking and thinking, behold they just gave one double and twist and were gone!

Now this had happened three nights one after the other. Three nights, one after the other, Idle had gone out, promising to bring in a sheaf of rays; three nights, one after the other, she had come back yawning and empty-handed; and three nights, one after the other, she had been whipped and sent to bed without any supper.

The Fruit of Idleness.

As ill-luck would have it, there was just then going to be a Grand Ball at Elfin Court, and Old Woman had been commanded to spin a thousand and ten new gossamer robes of the choicest patterns for the occasion. She set up her wheel in the doorway of her Ash-Tree, utterly resolved that no Fairy should go to Court in shabby clothes if she could help it ; and, being in high good-humour, she gave Idle some honey to her breakfast, and began to spin. First she spun a few robes of a pink ground embroidered with fronds of moss ; then she spun a few more all shining like a moted sunbeam, and a few more of sky-blue lined with silver, and a few more of thistle-grey edged with scarlet. These were for the most distinguished Fairies about Fairy Queen's Court ; but for Fairy Queen herself, Old Woman said she must have a ray and a half gathered off the dew on the wild white roses that grew over the Enchanted Bower a mile away through the forest.

Now Old Woman, hard as she could spin, was not able to walk, because she was lame on her feet, and naughty as Idle had been for three nights, one after the

other, she was obliged to trust her again ;
but before she sent her out she spoke these
words to her in a very serious tone of
voice, and with one eye looking through
her big horn spectacles at the rod in the
corner which was used to whip Idle when
she came home empty-handed—

"Now, Idle, hearken to me," was her
solemn commencement ; "you have not
far to go nor much to carry, and you
must on no account sit down to rest ; for
to-night the Wicked Fairy of the Creeping
Plant with many Tendrils is abroad, and
he will catch you if you do. Perhaps he
will kill you ; but even if he does not kill
you he will tie you hand and foot and
keep you a prisoner as long as you live.
Now remember what I say, and run away
and be a good Idle ! "

So Idle primmed herself up, and put on
her shoes, and went out in the finest
intentions. "I'll be as quick as Trip, as
clever as Try-for-it," thought she ; but as
she crossed the threshold one of her shoes

Idle is idle still.

fell off, and she did not stay to put it on again, because it would have been so much trouble to stoop, but went forward till she was out of sight of the cottage made in the hollow of the Ash-Tree, keeping always on the edge of the soft turf by the way-side, and chirping over and over to herself how good she was going to be. This chirping presently put her out of breath, and she ceased to walk so fast; also she began to feel the stones in the turf, and to wish she had not lost her shoe.

"It is only a mile, however," said she; "and I have plenty of time. The stars will shine till cock-crowing, and it's only a mile!"

When she had made out how short a way she had to go, Idle thought she might as well not fatigue herself. The wild white roses on the Enchanted Bower would be there all the same, with the dew upon them and the rays in their hearts, if she enjoyed herself a little bit, as they would if she hurried and tired herself ever so much. And who would know ? Not Old Woman, for she had left her spinning green coats for Tippety Wichet and his brothers, and they were not likely to be finished until long after she could get home again.

"And as for the Wicked Fairy of the Creeping Plant with many Tendrils," said Idle, lying down comfortably on a mossy bank, " I don't believe in him one bit ; so here I shall stay and have a nice pleasant nap."

Idle's Dis= belief.

In a very few minutes the little silly thing was fast asleep, and Old Woman, spinning at the doorway of her house in the hollow of the Ash-Tree, had finished Tippety Wichet's coat, and his brother's too, long before she woke again.

Now if Idle had looked up at the tree which overshadowed the mossy bank before she lay down, she would have seen a most strange and horrible sight. She would have seen a wizened, monkey-faced creature perched at the end of one of the branches, grinning from ear to ear.

Idle is caught by the Wicked Fairy.

He was very still until Idle shut her eyes, and then he began to toss himself over and over, and up and down, and backwards and forwards, but always holding on to the end of the branch; and when Idle gave her first snore (Idle always snored, which was not pretty in a little maid), he chuckled and laughed, "Hee, hee! hi, hi! ho, ho!" until you would have thought he must strangle himself. But he did not. He only chuckled again, and then crowed out triumphantly, "I've got her! I've got her! I've got her! Little Idle, Old Woman's Maid!" until from every flower-cup, and every pebble, and every cushion of moss, started up the Elves and Sprites, all curious to see what there was to do.

They ought to have been sorry for Idle when they saw her lying asleep under the tree where lived the Wicked Fairy of the Creeping Plant with many Tendrils; but she had been such a dull, tiresome Idle all her life, that they had no pity left for her ; and they only chuckled and laughed and crowed too, until the forest was all alive with their fun ; and Old Woman, waiting at her door in the hollow of the Ash-Tree, with Tippety Wichet's finished coat in her lap, wondered what was the matter, and said, " Could that naughty Idle have fallen into trouble again ? "

Idleness breeds Contempt.

But into whatever trouble Idle might have fallen, Old Woman could not go to help her ; for, you know, she was lame of her feet and could not walk ; so she only sighed, and began to spin more coats ; and this time, having no rays for trimmings, she used white cats' whiskers, which were rather stiff, but made a variety. Idle therefore slept and snored on until the stars winked themselves out, and neither ray nor dew was left upon the wild white roses that overgrew the Enchanted Bower. It was quite chill and shivery when she awoke, and the grey colour of the morning before the sun is risen was amongst the trees.

Idle's Awakening.

"Oh, dear! what shall I do?" cried Idle. "I have nothing to carry home. Old Woman will whip me again, and Fairy Queen will have to go to the Ball in an old gown!"

When Idle made this lamentation, there was a spiteful little giggle up in the tree, and the Wicked Fairy of the Creeping Plant with many Tendrils threw down a fat snail on her face, which made her give a great spring to get away. But directly she did that, she found that she was tied fast, hand and foot, flat on her back, and the monkeyfied creature on the branch sang out, "I've caught you, Idle, though you didn't believe in me one bit. I've caught you, and you can't get away;" as if he would only have liked to see her try.

For a little while Idle lay still and dismally afraid, with the shiny black snail crawling all over her face; for she could not shake her head to throw it off, or get so much as a finger free to poke it away.

She is bound by Chains of her own Making

She kept her mouth screwed up, and her
eyes tight shut, and felt all over such a
dreadful weight, as if in her sleep she had
been taken out of her own body and put
into one as big as that of Giant Slouchback ; but when she had been some time
quiet, she peeped and saw that she was
no larger than when Old Woman sent her
out the night before to gather the rays
for Fairy Queen's ball-dress : what made
her unable to stir was that thousands of
the Tendrils of a great Creeping Plant
that grew out of the roots of the tree
were twined about her limbs. Her ankles
were bound together by them, and her
hands were fastened to her sides; round
each of her fingers there was a score of
rings at least, and so twined, twisted,
and knotted, that nobody but the ugly,
wicked Fairy who twined, twisted, and
knotted them, could ever unloose them
again. Idle fancied they did not look
very strong ; but when she tried to break
them, she found they were as tough as

From
which
there is
no Es=
caping.

whipcord, and, besides, had little pricks all over them that stung her like wasps whenever she attempted to move. So, at last, she gave up trying, and let the nasty fat black snail crawl over her and cover her with slime.

The Wicked
Fairy's
Delight.

The Wicked Fairy laughed and shouted with glee at the sight, and pelted her with slugs and caterpillars and damp red worms, until the Elves and Sprites, who dislike ugly things, were fain to run away and leave Idle to her punishment. Then the cold frogs and toads began to hop over her and croak at her, and the young nettles and briars amongst the moss, and the Tendrils of the Creeping Plant, grew up so fast before noon, that the good folks passing by that way could not see Idle tied down amongst them.

And when Old Woman found that she did not return, she got another little Maid, whose name was Brisk, who served her much better than Idle had ever done, and who was a great favourite with the

Fairies, because she was a little Maid of
wonderful taste and imagination. By her
help Old Woman had all the new Court
dresses ready in time for the Grand Ball;
the chief novelties, besides Fairy Queen's
royal robes of silver rays and carnation,
being white lily-bells for her Majesty's
four-and-twenty Maids of Honour, and
blue jerkins and scarlet stockings for the
four-and-twenty Court Pages.

Little
Maid
Brisk.

FAIRY QUEEN'S HERALDS PROCLAIM
the GRAND BALL at ELFIN COURT

ONE beautiful morning, at the beginning of Midsummer days, Fairy
Tippet and Fairy Wink were enjoying themselves in a long gossip under
the shadow of a mushroom, when they
saw the Queen's Heralds coming, and
heard the great sound of trumpeting which
always preceded their advance ; so they
sprang upon the top of the mushroom, to
get a grand view of the Royal Procession.

First came twelve banner-bearers, bearing
banners of poppy-silk ; then the Chief
Herald, whose name of state was the
Grand Pomp, in a scarlet cloak and flap

14

A great
Sound
of Trum=
peting.

hat, his assistant heralds, Trig and Tart, one on each side of him, carrying copies of the Royal Proclamation.

Behind them followed three score and five trumpeters, with trumpets of golden reeds, through which, at the entrance of every glade, and on the top of every hill, they blew a blast, long, loud, and shrill. Three times, with a pause between, they blew a blast, long, loud, and shrill, and then the Grand Pomp drew himself up, and read the Royal Proclamation.

Fairy Queen's Ball.

" To all Sheneland, to all Fairies, Elves, and Sprites, by the Queen's courtesy, greeting. Come to the Ball! Come! come ! ! come ! ! ! "

After which, the three score and five trumpeters blew another blast, long, loud, and shrill, and the Royal Procession moved on. Tippet and Wink bowed most respectfully as the Grand Pomp passed by the mushroom on which they were perched, and kept profound silence until the last of the trumpeters was out of sight, when they immediately began to discuss the coming event.

" Of course, Tippet, *you* will go," said Wink, wriggling with joyous vanity at the prospect of appearing at Elfin Court Ball, for he was young, and had never been bidden to one before.

Tippet replied carelessly, that he did not know—he had attended so many. He was there the last time, and had found very little intellectual amusement indeed. *The* event of the evening was Tricksy's tumble into the trifle, when he got up to return thanks for his wife Sweet-lips' health having been drunk at supper.

Wink had never heard of it ! Oh, *would* Tippet tell him ?

Tippet said he felt scruples. As a rule, he disapproved of gossip, and thought that what passed at Fairy Queen's table ought not to be made the subject of common conversation ; but as Wink was his *particular* friend, and young and inex-

perienced besides, he would just tell *him*.
Perhaps it might be a *lesson* to him.

"It appears," began Tippet, in the
dignified narrative manner of one who
knows he has something worth hearing
to relate; "it appears that when Tricksy
and Sweet-lips were presented to Fairy
Queen, on the occasion of their happy
and auspicious union, her Majesty had
graciously promised Tricksy that his
lovely bride should sit on the Daïs of
Beauty, at her right hand, at the supper
of the coming ball. Imagine Tricksy's elation; it quite lifted him off his balance!
Between the presentation and the Ball,
I never met him, I give you my honour,
that he was not walking on tiptoe, with his
little cocked nose in the air, so that he
could not behold your humble servant.

But we all know the upshot of Court
favours! I am proud to say that I owe
my country *nothing*. My services may
have been *great*, but——"

"Don't be tedious, Tippet," interposed

2

the audacious Wink, deprecatingly ; so
the ancient courtier smiled, sighed, and
again took up the thread of his story.

" My dancing days are over, though I
have footed it amongst the lightest, and
I have almost lost my relish for the dainty
ceremonials of supper ; but when the
trumpets blew, and Grand Pomp marshalled
the way for the Queen and her Ladies,
I followed with the stream, and soon
saw that Sweet-lips was duly placed on
her Gracious Majesty's right hand. It is
impossible, Wink, to say which was the
lovelier. The Queen wore her crown and
royal robes of rich colours, but Sweet-
lips was all in white, as pure as herself ;
and I do consider, *between you and me*,
that she might have made a better choice
than of the pert fellow Tricksy."

In this confidential observation Wink perfectly coincided, but not with reference to
Tippet individually ; for all Sheneland knew
that Tippet had had no success in his woo-
ings, and that he remained a bachelor solely

because no fairy, except one of the three sisters, Snip, Snap, and Snarl, would have him, and he could not make up his mind to try any of them *yet*.

" The fellow," Tippet went on scornfully, referring to Tricksy—" the fellow, as usual, looked like a harlequin, and close at his elbow were Quip and Crank, every moment prompting him to do or say some mad thing or other. I sat on pins and needles, for there was no knowing if even the Queen's own Fairy Majesty would be safe from his unseemly antics. However, the Queen overlooked them, and once or twice condescended to laugh merrily at what he said, though, I confess, the jest seemed but poor to *me* ; and at length Muffin, the Royal Master of the Ceremonies, by the Queen's command, ordered us to charge our glasses, and drink the health of the sweetest bride and most gallant groom that Sheneland had beheld since the last marriage at Elfin Court.

Quip and Crank.

" It was done ; the cheering died into silence. Sweet-lips dropt a modest ' Thank you ' ; and I was congratulating myself *that* bore was over, when it occurred to Tricksy that here was an opportunity of distinguishing himself, and you know, Wink, whether *he* is the sort of fellow to let it slip. He stood up—on tiptoe, as little fellows always do—and leaned his fingers on the table, bending them so far back, in his nervous efforts to be smart, that it made me wretched to watch them ; and stretching forward so far, that I thought he wanted to knock his head against his opposite neighbour's. I knew he would come to grief from the beginning, but I cannot say that I felt really sorry for him when, in the difficult agonies of his elo- quence, his legs slipped from under him, and he fell face foremost into a dish of trifle ! But I pitied Sweet-lips, I did indeed, Wink. Tricksy was carried out by Quip and Crank, moaning grievously ; but that was mere make-believe. We all

knew he couldn't be *hurt*, though he raised
such a sympathy amongst the ladies.
Indeed, if one must be a fool, and fall
with one's face into anything, trifle is
excellent for the purpose. At the accident
our Gracious Queen herself deigned to
express concern. She was eating oyster
at the time."

Wink seemed glad to hear it, and remarked that oyster in moderation was a
capital thing. At which Tippet shuddered,
and replied that the pleasures of the table
were nothing to him now, he had such a
shocking digestion ; and that subject once
broached by the elderly sufferer, there is
no saying how long it might have lasted,
had not the fashionable promenade, by
which grew the mushroom where the
gossips sat, suddenly become thronged
with all the youth, beauty, and wit of
Sheneland.

There was but one theme of conversation
and discussion throughout the gay assemblage, and that was, of course, the coming

The Gay
Assem-
blage
of
Shene-
land

Discuss
the
Coming
Ball.

Ball at Elfin Court. Tippet and Wink recognised their friends, and mingled in the crowd. Tippet was a notorious old scandal-monger, and many dowager Fairies liked a chat with him on things in general ; and Wink was a young spark who was only just beginning to be tolerated, for many persons of taste said that his manners were forward and flippant, without the pleasing innocence of Tricksy. However, each met a welcome ; and while Tippet was gossiping with Wrinkle and Sneer, Wink attached himself to a bevy of pretty Elves, who were flirting their rose-leaf parasols in the sunshine, and prattling the dearest nonsense ; and he made himself so agreeable, that Elf Bluebell promised him the first dance with her at Elfin Court Ball— a promise which he confided with much affectation of secrecy to every male individual of his acquaintance before the afternoon was half over, and they said he was a conceited Wink, and gave himself airs.

And while the fashionable promenade was still crowded, the Royal Procession of Heralds, Banner-bearers, and Trumpeters returned from sounding the Queen's Proclamation throughout Sheneland; and a way was made for them to pass through in the deepest silence; and when the Grand Pomp reached the Sun Pavilion, at the top of the walk, he faced about, the banners were waved, the trumpets blew a blast, long, loud, and shrill, and Trig and Tart read the Proclamation thrice over.

The Royal Proclamation.

" To all Sheneland, to all Fairies, Elves, and Sprites, by the Queen's courtesy, greeting. Come to the Ball! Come! come!! come!!! "

And when that was done, the banners were lowered, and the Heralds' Procession disappeared from the respectful gaze of the people, within the golden gates of the Sun Pavilion.

The GRAND BALL at ELFIN COURT & WHAT HAPPENED THERE

WHEN the evening of the Grand Ball arrived, in every bower throughout Sheneland there was great fuss and jubilation; but Fairy Queen's bower saw by far the sweetest sight of all. There was Fairy Queen herself in her royal robes of carnation and silver rays, with a petticoat of gossamer, and a crown of diamond dew-sparkles on her head. Around her were her four-and-twenty Maids of Honour, all clad alike in white lily-bells, and her four-and-twenty Pages, all clad alike in blue jerkins and scarlet stockings.

To the sound of the trumpets, and with

24

the Grand Pomp strutting stage-fashion
before her, Fairy Queen, with her Prime
Minister, Prince Goldheart, on her right
hand, and all her Court filed in graceful
procession up the Great Hall of Dancing,
where the company was assembled, and
only waiting for her Majesty's arrival to
open the revels. The guests made their
profoundest reverences, and then Muffin,
the Master of the Ceremonies, clapped his
hands thrice; upon which the music struck
up, and the four-and-twenty Maids of Honour in lily-bells immediately paired off with
the four-and-twenty Pages in blue jerkins
and scarlet stockings, as a signal that the
rest of the company might begin to dance.

The Ball commences.

Fairy Queen sat on a throne on the Daïs
of Beauty, admiring everything and conversing affably with whomsoever approached
her, thus making herself popular, and
winning golden opinions from all her faithful subjects. She bowed to Tippet in
recognition of his original remark that it
had been a fine day, and he went about

Sheneland all the rest of his life as a Fairy of Distinction, because he said he had been permitted to make a confidential communication to the Queen.

Wink, Trip, Try-for-it, Frolic, Finick, Turn, Twist, Lush, and Trap, danced with Bluebell, Satin, Sleek, Sly, Flip, Arch, Mite, Dot, and Dimple, and a very pretty dance it was ; for they were all gay young Fairies, with light heads and light heels, who knew nothing of the cares of life, except by hearsay. Tricksy and Sweet-lips did not dance, because they were staid married people ; but Sly whispered it about that Tricksy's feet were going under the bench to the tune of the music, all the while he was sitting so demure by his wife.

Tippety Wichet and his Brothers, by Fairy Queen's express wish, danced with the three ugly Elves, Snip, Snap, and Snarl ; for her Majesty had benignly remarked that at Court *courtesy* should prevail, and that it hurt her to see those who were plain or out of date rudely

Courtesy prevails.

THE·BALL·WENT
ON·JOYOUSLY

neglected for the younger and prettier faces. But after that penitential hop, Tippety Wichet and his Brothers were at liberty to choose for themselves; and they danced with Posy, Dove, and Poppet, three lovely sister Elves, who made their first appearance that night.

The Ball went on joyously, and everybody was in a state of extreme enjoyment, when Muffin clapped his fat hands thrice, the instruments of music became suddenly silent, the trumpets sounded, and the Grand Pomp bounced in much flustered, and mumbled out some announcement which nobody quite heard. Then appeared a lean, little, old Fairy, with enormous long legs, hidden under a sweeping green train of ferns, who was a perfect stranger at Court, though, from her haughty self-possession, you might have thought she had been there every day of her life since she was born.

A Stranger Fairy enters.

Fairy Queen looked dignified and astonished, and begged the Grand Chamberlain,

Enquiry
is
made
concern=
ing her.

who stood behind her throne, to discover the style and title of that Lady who had entered her presence with the assumption of royal state ; but the Grand Pomp had quite lost his presence of mind, and did not remember anything but what sounded like the hiss of a serpent when the stranger spoke to give her name.

While the inquiry was pending, the lean, little, old Fairy, with the enormous long legs, advanced straight up to the steps of the Daïs of Beauty, paused before Fairy Queen, and bowed condescendingly. Fairy Queen consulted her dignity, and bowed in the same manner, and the company began to whisper all round and to titter respectfully in remote corners and behind pillars. The stranger did not seem to take it amiss ; she looked over the heads of the crowd, curled her lips, showed her teeth, and scowled at them, but nothing more. Sneer and Scandal said they believed they had seen her somewhere before, but they were in no hurry to claim her acquaintance, and she did not seem to have a single friend in the room.

Fairy Queen, to do the honours of her Court, begged her to be seated, but the stranger declined ; she could not *sit*, she was obliged to her Majesty. Would she dance, then ? She could not *dance*, she was obliged to her Majesty. So she was permitted to stand by the wall, and look grand, without being any more notice taken of, except by Tippet and Wink, who got into her immediate vicinity and jealously watched for some accident to the fern train which might reveal the secret of her enormous length of leg.

The Fairy had a sharp face and a watchful expression of uneasiness upon it, as if she expected from moment to moment to be shocked by some unpleasant spectacle. Especially she kept an eye on the doorway, and when there was a little bustle and hum about it, as of admiration and surprise, she raised herself up so that Tippet and Wink saw two wooden pegs under her fern

train with which she had gracefully eked
out her own short limbs. They immediately
told Whisper, who set it about the room
that the late distinguished arrival was a
Fairy with wooden legs ! This intelligence,
following close upon the sensations of
jealousy, wonder, and awe which her assumption of royal state had excited, could not
fail to create a feeling of general satisfaction ;
but even that gave way before the delight
that seized upon everybody when the
trumpets blew again, and the Grand Pomp
announced, in the midst of a profound
silence, " Prince Glee and Princess Trill."

Their appearance was as sudden as it
was unexpected, and the multitude could
not repress their cheers of welcome.   Prince
Glee was Fairy Queen's own cousin, and
Princess Trill was the lovely niece of a
despotic and malicious old Fairy, who had
for many years kept herself aloof from Court
because she had been refused a place about
her Gracious Majesty's person when she
ascended the throne of Sheneland. She

was quite welcome to enjoy her solitude and dulness, if she preferred them, for she was exceedingly mischievous and disagreeable ; but all the world cried shame upon her when she snatched Princess Trill away from the innocent pleasures of Elfin Court, and proclaimed her right and authority to immure that young and happy creature in any one of her own dreary residences, to keep her safe from the vanities and temptations of Elfin-Life. Princess Trill wept bitterly, and entreated to be allowed to remain with her companions, the Queen's Maids of Honour, or, at least, to take leave of them, and give them messages of farewell to Prince Glee, who loved her.

But her Aunt flew into a passion, and refused her every grace, and immediately poor Princess Trill was shut up in the ugly pumpkin coach, and carried away nobody knew whither. When this cruel event happened, Prince Glee was absent from Court on a mission for his cousin the Queen, whose most trusted envoy he had been

The history of Princess Trill.

She is carried away by Wicked Aunt.

ever since her accession to the crown ; but as soon as he returned there were innumerable friends waiting to tell him the disastrous news about Princess Trill. At first he turned very pale, then he turned very red, but when he was calm again he cried, " Never will I sleep on thistledown again until I find that sweet, persecuted Princess, and deliver her from captivity."

At which the whole assembly applauded, and six young Knights-Fairy of the Royal Guard volunteered themselves as his companions, by the Queen's own gracious sympathy and permission.

And immediately they set off, travelling night and day, and running into many perils, but always getting safe out of them, though they could hear no tidings of Princess Trill, which saddened them all inexpressibly. They had been three months away, and were still on their bootless journeyings, when they encountered the Queen's Heralds proclaiming the Grand

Ball at Elfin Court, and the six young
Knights-Fairy said they would not miss it
for the world. So Prince Glee gave them
leave to go home, but he continued his
travels ; for he had no heart to enjoy
himself while his dear Princess Trill was
held in durance. The Knights-Fairy carried
their sad news of failure back to Court,
and gave it as their opinion that her Aunt
had *drowned* the lovely Princess, and that
Prince Glee would never see her more
unless he went out of Sheneland and
into the Water-World himself.

Imagine, then, the great joy and elation
felt by all the guests at the Ball, when the
Grand Pomp announced, in his biggest
voice—

" Prince Glee and Princess Trill ! "

The crowd pressed forward, and beheld
the sweet Princess all one rosy blush under
her veil ; and Muffin, Master of the Ceremonies, came bowing and scraping his
loose left leg to lead them to the Daïs
of Beauty where Fairy Queen was waiting

3

to welcome them. The dancing ceased ;
but the music played a fine march while
all the company fell into rank, right and
left, to see the Prince and Princess walk
up to the Daïs, with Muffin smiling on
them like a full moon.

The Stranger Fairy is excited

Amongst those whose curiosity was the
most excited was the lean, little, old
Fairy with wooden legs and a fern train.
Craning forward her head, she beheld
Princess Trill, and Prince Glee leading
her by the hand. Her face turned green,
she gasped for breath, and would have
rushed forward to separate them had not
that spirit of mischief, Crank, put his
foot in her way just in the nick of time.
She stumbled against it, tripped, and fell
flat across the space left by the company—
full in front of the Queen, of Muffin, and

And Trips and Falls,

of the Prince and Princess ; tearing her
fern train to ribbons, and in her fall dis-
playing the two stout wooden pegs on
which she had tried to exalt herself above
the heads of all Elfin Court.

Everybody else smiled, but Princess Trill, full of terror, cried out, " My Aunt Spite ! my Aunt Spite ! " and clung to the Prince for protection ; but when the wicked old Fairy did not attempt to rise, her tender heart was touched, and she exclaimed, " Woe is me, for she is dead ! she is dead ! "

Revealing her Identity

But the great Court Doctor Pille declared that she was nothing like it ; and some young fellows having carried her out to the air, she was presently brought to under the Royal Pump, and then given in charge to Catch and Keep, the Queen's head-jailers, until it was determined what punishment she had incurred by her miserable behaviour.

This painful incident occupied but a few minutes, and Princess Trill forgot it immediately the Queen took her hand, called her " Fair Cousin," kissed her, and made her sit by her on the Daïs of Beauty, with Prince Glee on the other side. Then her Majesty was graciously pleased to

With Aunt Spite.

be curious about their adventures, and silence being proclaimed, the Prince related them.

"Your Majesty has heard all that happened before the six young Knights-Fairy left me to return to Elfin Court Ball," he began, "and therefore I will resume the thread of my narrative where it was broken off. Being left alone I wandered on until I came to a vast building which appeared to have the smallest windows in Sheneland, and no door at all. I knew in a moment that I had discovered Castle Craft, and while I was sorrowfully surveying its grim walls I heard a sound which, at first, I mistook for the cry of a bird, but listening a little longer, I recognised it as the voice of Princess Trill, weeping and wailing in her cruel captivity. I was immediately furnished with magical strength; I stormed the castle single-handed, flung open the secret gates, slew Lies and Fibs, the guards, and penetrated to the secret chambers, where I found

many prisoners wearing life away in the dreariest state you can imagine. Them I set free, and afterwards I fought my way up to the highest chamber of a dismal tower, and there, immured in darkness, I found the sweet Princess. She sprang towards me, I bore her down the stair, and mounting my favourite steed, Swift-and-Sure, we fled from the domains of Castle Craft, and arrived here in time for the Ball. Fortunately for us, Aunt Spite had gone abroad that evening on a mission of malice regarding other persons, or doubtless she would have impeded our escape. Finding the Princess gone on her return to Castle Craft, she has followed us here with rage in her wicked heart to separate us ; but she will never succeed ! "

And sweet Princess Trill smiled happily, and repeated " *Never !* "

Fairy Queen was charmed with her Cousin's story, and as soon as it was finished all the guests went in to supper, where Muffin, by her Majesty's command, pro-

He bears Princess Trill away.

Princess Trill's Answer.

posed the health of Prince Glee and Princess Trill. It was drunk standing, with nine times nine cheers; after which the company shivered their glasses, that they might never serve a meaner purpose.

Then Prince Glee made a short but beautiful speech, which even Tippet applauded; and Wink made the remark to pretty little Dot, who sat beside him, that he should know what to say *now* when *he* stood in Glee's shoes; which Dot interpreted to her own satisfaction, and smiled and blushed accordingly.

And both Ball and supper went off so well that Fairy Queen was highly gratified; and as soon as she was sleepy, Muffin nodded his head thrice, and softly clapped his fat hands. Then all the lights at Elfin Court were put out, and everybody went home to bed.

And the next day the Queen issued her Royal mandate that henceforward Spite should be banished from Sheneland for

ever. Wink, Quip, Crank, Trap, Catch
and Keep were ordered to escort her to the
frontier ; and in such wild company I leave
you to imagine whether she had a pleasant
journey or not.

THE SOLEMN FESTIVAL OF MIDSUMMER EVE

MIDSUMMER EVE is a very great and solemn Festival in Sheneland.

Between Sunset and Moonrise all Elfin Court goes out in procession, with Fairy Queen, to the Enchanted Bower in the midst of Elfinwood. Torches are carried before them by the Gnomes who work in the Mines, to light the path which winds, and turns, and twists, through a bewildering labyrinth for miles and miles. The procession is made in perfect silence, and all the way as the Fairies go they pluck flowers, weeds, herbs, and branches ; never pausing, never stooping, never speaking,

and never looking either to the right hand
or to the left. As they pass into the
Enchanted Bower they cast them all
down into one heap by the door, and then
range themselves mutely round the garlanded walls, while Fairy Queen takes her
seat on the Golden Throne in the midst.

All is so still that the chirp of the insects To the Music of the Lily-bells.
which wake by night in Elfinwood is heard
like a chorus of music, mingled with the
chiming of blue-bells and lily-bells in the
moist and shady places. Suddenly the
inner gate of the Enchanted Bower opens,
and a cold breath blows softly through ;
then there is a sound as of trailing robes
over crisp leaves in autumn, and then
appears a misty figure whose face is covered
with a veil. She moves like a shadow,
diffusing all around her a chill air, and
takes her place beside the heap of flowers,
weeds, herbs, and branches, which the
Fairies gathered by the way and flung
down in a heap at the entrance of the
Enchanted Bower.

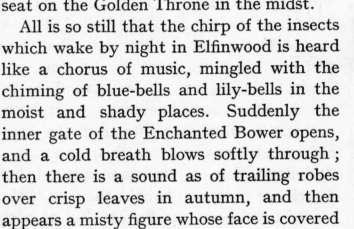

As she comes forth, the Moon rises and the Stars twinkle out one by one ; and just as the Fairy Bells chime midnight all Elfinwood echoes to the rush and hurry of light feet,—not fairy feet, but feet of maidens from the Country under the Sun, who, on Midsummer Eve, come out to Sheneland, to inquire of the Veiled Shadow of the Future what their fate shall be ; and on this night, once in the year, she draws their lot, and shows it to them by the emblem of some one flower, weed, herb, or branch, which she lifts from the heap at her feet, and gives into their hands.

Fright‑ ened Mortal Maidens come

Neither Fairy Queen nor any of her Court has power to behold the face of the Veiled Shadow of the Future, but as each young maiden draws near to learn her fate, *she* sees it for a moment, but for a moment only. In that moment, however, each maiden's countenance becomes a perfect reflex of the Veiled Face ; and the Fairies standing round the garlanded walls, and Fairy Queen seated on her Golden Throne

and see the Veiled Face of the Future.

The
Fairies
knew
she had
received
a Thorn
in her
heart.

in the midst, can see thereby whether there is bliss or bane, weal or woe, joy or dole, in store for each of them.

On the Midsummer Eve following the great Ball at Elfin Court, Fairy Queen and all the Court went in Procession, as usual, through the Labyrinth, from the Palace to the Enchanted Bower, and, in due order, the Fate-drawing began.

First, there came up a dark-eyed damsel, with ripe cheeks, and lovely white arms— her lips warm with laughter, and her eyes bright with Love and Happiness. She paused on the outer edge of the circle of cold air that environed the Veiled Figure, and looked steadfastly upon her face. Then her own changed suddenly; her lips paled, her eyes stared haggardly; all the bloom faded from her cheeks; her white arms fell, then clasped themselves passionately across her breast. And so the Fairies knew that she had received a *thorn* in her heart.

A Thorn-pierced Little Maiden.

The next was a pale, fair maiden, drooping and tender, with no lustre either in her eyes or her smile ; and as she looked up in the face of the Veiled Figure her own grew blank as a shadow on the wall, and so faded back, crowned with *everlastings*, into the night.

Love's Magic.

The third was very young and timid. Scarcely dared she approach ; and when she did, it was but to glance one hurried instant at the magical face, and then to fly off, blushing like the morning, with wealth of *roses, myrtles, and orange-bloom* clasped in her arms.

She was followed by a calm, little, gipsy-eyed creature, who turned to the Veiled Figure as if she were only half-curious to learn what she could reveal ; but the first glance struck her with a pang of such anguish as shivered her glassy quiet into fragments, and, passing, left her features seamed and wrinkled, and still again, like a plain where there has been earthquake. A branch of *deadly nightshade* was clutched in her lean hands.

Then appeared a cold, proud maiden, in rich and rare apparel, who beheld the Veiled Figure with a smile of defiance; but it changed into a tortured expression of pain and humiliation, as a bunch of *sour sorrel* was laid on her outstretched palm.

The next was a buxom lassie, with a countenance like May sunshine, and on her the Veiled Figure smiled, for her face bloomed into full summer as she took a *palm branch and olive branch, and her arms full of figs and grapes.*

A peep into the Future.

Her successor was a shrewish, sour, discontented maiden, who looked all the crosser for being stung by the *nettles*, which the Veiled Figure gave her; and her sister, who came next, and received a *bramble*, was not much pleasanter to see.

The drawing of the lots could only go on from Midnight until the first hour of the morning; and as the last minutes flew by there was great crowding round the entrance of the Enchanted Bower, and eager hands outstretched to the Veiled Figure for their emblem of Fate. And one maiden got *thrift*, for labour ; and another *moss*, for lowliness ; and a third *ivy*, for constancy ; and a fourth *wheat*, for usefulness. And when the Fairy Bells chimed One, all the maidens rushed away from Sheneland to their own Country under the Sun.

Then the Veiled Figure retired within the inner gate of the Enchanted Bower, and Fairy Queen's silent procession trooped back to Elfin Court.

THERE'S NO SMOKE WHERE
THERE'S NO FIRE

WHEN this solemn Festival of Midsummer Eve was over, Fairy
Queen and her Court left the Palace in
Elfinwood, and went away to the sea,
where her Majesty had an Air-Palace,
built in a beautiful wooded chine of the
rocks, and garlanded all over with roses.

Now it was to this frontier of Sheneland
that Spite had been exiled, and immediately
the Court arrived at the Air-Palace she
renewed her correspondence with her
secret friends who travelled in the Royal
suite. Slander, Gossip, Idlewords, and
Sneer were very glad to get her letters;

Spite
and her
Friends

47

and Twaddle, who was considered a well-meaning, though foolish, person, began to run about and say what a misunderstood and persecuted character Spite was, and to urge that she should be permitted to **Concoct a** return to Sheneland. Finally, she got up **Petition.** a petition, which was numerously signed by the Court supernumeraries and others, and on a set day it was presented to Fairy Queen by Spite's friends and allies.

Her Gracious Majesty, whose character for clemency was well known, gave this petition which Mischief, an unacknowledged daughter of Spite's, had written out, her best consideration. She also took the advice of Prince Goldheart upon it ; but as she was inclined to the side of mercy, he did not press for a perpetual exile, much as his judgment would have approved it. And so the first sentence was quashed,  and a Queen's Messenger was sent off to tell Spite that she might cross the border again and dwell in Sheneland, providing she kept away from Court, and held her wicked tongue in good order. To which conditions Spite readily agreed, and returned to Sheneland the same afternoon.

Those persons who had been instrumental in procuring her pardon received her with triumph ; but Prince Glee and Princess Trill, the four-and-twenty Maids of Honour, all the Pages, the Knights-Fairy of the Royal Guard, and many others beside, were extremely sorry to hear of her return : for they knew that as soon as Spite and Mischief and their favourite companions met, their machinations would begin. And so, of course, they did.

The very next morning, Spite, the mother of Mischief, Mischief herself, Slander, Sneer, Idlewords, Gossip, and Twaddle met together on the seashore not far from the Royal Landing Place. Her Majesty's yacht, a lovely pearl and pink shell, was moored at the steps in the midst of a gay little fleet, waiting to carry Fairy Queen and her Court on a summer day's sail to the Isle of Palms. None of Spite's friends

Mischief Brewing.

4

had been invited to attend, for they were almost as much out of favour as herself, because of the frequent quarrels they caused amongst Fairy Queen's otherwise loyal and well-disposed subjects.

This was their way of proceeding : Spite said ill-natured things, which Slander magnified, and Gossip repeated ; then Idlewords made silly comments, Sneer looked unutterable things, and Twaddle talked *goody*, until amongst them they had kindled up a nice, brisk fire, which Mischief never allowed to die out for want of stirring.

Now Spite, though she was in reality own mother to Mischief, always pretended not to know her, and called her publicly an arrogant and presuming young person ; for you must understand that Spite tried her utmost to seem respectable, and often insisted on claiming relationship with Justice and Truth, which Justice and Truth refused to acknowledge quite as peremptorily as she refused to acknowledge her own ugly and disagreeable daughter, Mischief.

Spite and those friends of hers whom you know, had all met together by appointment on the seashore to watch Fairy Queen and her Court embark, and while they were waiting they thus entered into conversation.

"What a lamentable circumstance it is!" began Spite, to whom all the others listened with veneration; "what a truly lamentable circumstance that Prince Glee, in the midst of his feigned passion for the Princess Trill, should have fallen into such an infatuated fondness for Clipsome, her Majesty's new Maid of Honour; she is but a flighty creature, and will not, I fear, prove a very desirable acquisition to our excellent Queen's train."

"Oh! has Prince Glee fallen in love with Clipsome? How jealous Princess Trill will be!" cried Idlewords.

"And it is said that he pays marked attention to Touchy as well," added

The Accusation against Prince Glee and

Slander ; and Sneer silently affirmed the same.

" Then his behaviour is highly incorrect !" exclaimed Twaddle. " It is very well known that her Majesty disapproves of the Royal Princes admiring her Maids of Honour. His conduct is most insincere, most inconstant ! But I never had any opinion of Prince Glee. There was no stability about him ; but it is disgraceful that he should transfer his assiduities from one to another as he does. Princess Trill loved him, but I suppose he is too weak to resist the attractions of Clipsome's fresh face. I don't think much of Touchy ; she is always off and on with somebody."

The Jealousy of his Detractors.

" Clipsome is not reported to be any great beauty," remarked Gossip ; " neither, for that matter, is poor Princess Trill. Her voice is *her* chief attraction. But Prince Glee never was noted for elegant taste ; his country breeding clings to him still ; and I have heard it quoted as a sentiment of his, that it is *far better* to be merry and happy, than to be ever so rich and great."

"Odious things!" cried Mischief, without circumlocution; "let us make them a fire and smoke them till they are as black as Gnomes! Who are they that they should go about enjoying themselves while we are left behind to catch sand-flies?"

Spite pretended not to have heard this last exclamation, but, in fact, it was she who had suggested it to her amiable daughter; and forthwith she set about picking up sticks until she had got a bigger faggot than anybody; and when they had all gathered as many as they could carry they brought their burdens and heaped them up on the shingle, and threw water over them, so that when they were kindled they might make a great smoke and cloud all over the sky above her Majesty's Air - Palace in the beautiful wooded chine of the rocks.

Mischief was for putting a spark to the pile immediately, but Spite slyly cautioned her to wait until they were by themselves,

Mischief is up to mischief

lest they should be detected, and made a pretence of sending Gossip, Slander, Sneer, Idlewords, and Twaddle away for more fuel, that they might not play spy and betray them. As soon as the five were out of hearing, Spite whispered, " *Now*," and gave a flint and steel to Mischief, who instantly struck a spark and dropped a bit of tinder on some crackling furze ; and then, while Spite blew gently to get it into a blaze, Mischief cried out to their friends to come and witness a real case of spontaneous combustion !

And they all gathered round in great delight and satisfaction, Twaddle saying how sad a pity it was that Prince Glee should not know better than to have two strings to his bow, and that if he would act so inconsistently he must expect to suffer. Idlewords added that Clipsome was as much to blame as Prince Glee for the encouragement she had given him ; and Slander suggested that in all probability Clipsome made the first advances with a

And Spite at work to spite.

Prince Glee and Clipsome.

view to supplant Princess Trill and vex
Touchy, who always fancied people admired
her, but was at the same time a proud
minx and easily offended. Gossip repeated
that no doubt the last suggestion was
the true one ; Clipsome was forward and
assuming, and took too much upon herself
by far, though any Fairy might see with half
a glance that her nose was slightly turned
up, that her mouth was wide, and that her
eyes were grey instead of blue.

" And as for her skin being fair," added
Twaddle, " why, her face is freckled like a
turkey's egg, and her figure is far more
buxom than elegant ! "

When
the
Grapes
are
Sour.

While they were still conversing in this
polite and pleasant manner, Muffin and the
Grand Pomp were seen coming down from
the Palace towards the steps of the landing-
place, with a Guard-Royal of fifty of her
Majesty's Knights-Fairy to keep the way,
and a band of musicians, who hurried to
their places in the Queen's Yacht and
immediately began to tune up. Scarcely

were they seated when the Queen herself, with Prince Goldheart and Prince Glee, appeared, followed by the Princesses, by Mother Dignity, the Mistress of the Robes, by the four-and-twenty Maids of Honour, and the four-and-twenty Pages, besides a miscellaneous crowd of Officials and People of Distinction then staying on a visit at the Air-Palace in the beautiful wooded chine of the rocks.

Now just as Fairy Queen and all her train passed down the shore, Mischief gave the freshly-kindled fire a stir, and suddenly a volume of ugly yellow smoke rolled over towards the royal party and grievously blackened Clipsome, Touchy, and Prince Glee ; blackened them so much that their pretty new clothes were all spoilt, and their faces darkened like those of the Gnomes who work in the mines.

Touchy began to cry, and Prince Glee flew into a great rage and fumed so noisily that Muffin was obliged to give him to understand that his conduct was contrary

The Fruits of Hate.

to Court etiquette, and that if he persisted in it he would have to be removed by the guard. Clipsome, however, was a Fairy of the highest spirit, and though young, she was clever, shrewd, and daring. She shook the grime off her robes as well as she could, and said to those of her companions who were near her—" It is Spite, Mischief, and Slander, who have a grudge against us because of Prince Glee and Princess Trill. But I defy them one and all!" which words being spoken very distinctly, reached the ears of Gossip, who forthwith repeated them to her friends, who chuckled, and said that Clipsome would not have been so venturesome as to defy them, had she known what an awful smoke they can make with a fire of their own kindling and tending.

The Cleverness of Clipsome.

Fairy Queen was so busy conversing with Prince Goldheart that this little incident did not attract her attention, but when she was seated under the awning of purple silk on board her Yacht, with all her Maids of

Honour grouped around her, she suddenly caught sight of Touchy's smeared face, and then of Clipsome's still more shady one. As for Prince Glee, Muffin had prevailed on him to get out of the way, and not to show himself at all. Her Majesty looked very grave, and beckoning to Mother Dignity, her Mistress of the Robes, requested her to discover why Touchy and Clipsome appeared in her presence in such unsightly trim.

The Queen's Indignation.

Immediately Mother Dignity began to make inquiries there were twenty voices ready to offer explanations. Clipsome was *so* careless, so almost *reckless* in her behaviour ; she depended on her fair face and good intentions until she forgot prudence ; and, in fact, though it was a matter to be much regretted, very hurtful things had been whispered against her and Prince Glee, and she was now showing the consequences of them in her begrimed robes and countenance. Touchy might be less to blame ; she was sharp with her tongue, and so made enemies, who had, perhaps, revenged themselves by inventing false and malicious reports against her. Mother Dignity, on hearing all this, looked very severely on Clipsome and Touchy, and communicated the results of her inquiries to the Queen.

Mother Dignity asserts her Authority.

Princess Trill, who sat by, heard it all with grief and astonishment, and though she could not believe a word against her brave and kind Prince Glee, who had rescued her from her Aunt Spite and the perils of Castle Craft, she let the tears roll down her lovely cheeks as she listened to Mother Dignity's report.

Now, hitherto, Clipsome had been a great favourite with her Royal Mistress. Though not a Princess or a person of title she came of a family of the very highest distinction in Sheneland; she was sprightly and well-bred, and of very gay and innocent manners. She could dance and sing better than any Fairy about Elfin Court except Princess Trill, but Prince Glee had only extolled

her skill just as Muffin and Grand Pomp might have done. As for Touchy, whatever he might have said to her was only in the way of fun, for he did not like her.

When, however, the Queen heard Mother Dignity's statement, she gazed with sorrowful severity on Clipsome, and she was bidden to approach the Royal Footstool, before which she stood, looking in the eyes of her companions and of all the Court the very image of a convicted culprit, for very few were clear-sighted enough to observe that the blackening of her features was not skin deep, and that she held her head erect and looked straight, honest, and innocent, out of her bright grey eyes.

" Clipsome," said the Queen, with gentle formality, " how comes it that thou art here in such unsightly guise ? Why are thy new gossamer robes all besmirched ? and why is thy visage darkened so foully ? "

" It is only Smoke, your Majesty," replied Clipsome, without hesitation.

The Queen was silent, but Mother Dignity

Clipsome and her Queen.

repeated with austere significance—"*Only Smoke*, Clipsome ? There's no smoke where there's no fire ! " And poor Clipsome's heart gave a great leap of indignation at finding herself mistrusted, and bowing hurriedly to her Royal Mistress she drew back quite out of sight, and spoke to none of her companions any more until they reached the Isle of Palms.

But when the Royal train landed, the Queen sent for her and said, as became her sweet majesty and gentleness—" Clipsome, I will not condemn thee unheard ; my heart inclines to thee. I have ever thought thy behaviour more noble than that of Prim, Prude, and Demure, who are the chief witnesses against thee ; but thy robes are much soiled, and either thou hast soiled them through carelessness thyself, or else some secret enemy has worked thee this malicious trick. I have spoken to Prince Glee, whose word is trusty as silver refined, but he is all smirched too, and poor Touchy has not escaped. I suspect a plot meant

cruelly to strike through thee at our dear Princess Trill. But be silent and patient; my officers, Pierce, Keen, Deep, and Farsight, are commissioned to search it out, and then I will hold a Court, and thou shalt be as publicly cleared, if innocent, as thou hast been publicly condemned now that appearances are so much against thee."

Clipsome's spirits still continued much depressed, but she drew a little comfort from the Queen's kind assurances. She would not share, however, in the dances and games under the Palm Trees, but went and sat down alone on the seashore, and sang mournfully to herself as the waves rolled in. Poor Princess Trill had likewise betaken herself to a hollow of the rocks out of sight, and was weeping in silence and solitude, when Prince Glee came down that way and found her. He was in a distracted mood, for he loved Princess Trill dearly, and she had never lifted her eyes or spoken to him once since the Queen's Yacht set sail for the Isle of Palms. He

The
Grief of
Clipsome
and
Princess
Trill,
and would have done or suffered anything for her sweet sake, and he was the last Fairy in all Sheneland to be false to his vows, or to seek to bring into disgrace such a pleasant Maid of Honour as Clipsome. He now drew near to Princess Trill, and knelt down at her feet ; at first he scarcely dared speak, but at length he gained courage to tell her it was all a mistake, and that he had *never* —NEVER—NEVER—loved anybody but herself, and as she did not repulse him, he consoled her with many kind words. And by and by they thought they would have a little walk along the shore, and as they went, they came up with Clipsome and with Touchy also, who had strayed away from the rest of the Queen's Maids of Honour in a most dolorous frame of mind.

The four persecuted Fairies then talked their troubles over, and Clipsome communicated to her companions in misfortune what the Queen had told her of a suspected plot ; and of Pierce, Keen, Deep, and Far-

Prince Glee's Consolation.

sight having been sent to search out the conspiracy. On that Princess Trill said, " If there be a plot, my Aunt Spite is at the bottom of it ; " and Prince Glee immediately cheered up, and cried that all would come right in the end, and that truth and justice never failed to triumph in the long run.

Merrily goes the Dance.

Meanwhile, the two-and-twenty Maids of Honour who were left with her Majesty danced with the Pages under the Palm Trees, and all the Court looked on ; and at noon there was a collation of sweets, cakes, and fruit ; after which there was more dancing, and some merry games of leap-frog and hop-scotch, in which Muffin and the Grand Pomp covered themselves with glory ; and as the sun went round to the west, the Royal train returned to the Queen's Yacht, and sailed away from the Isle of Palms to Sheneland, and the Air-Palace in the beautiful wooded chine of the rocks.

As the fleet approached the shore, Farsight being on the watch, saw thick black and yellow rolling clouds of smoke rising from a fire kindled on the beach, which darkened all the sky; next he discerned the seven wicked Fairies flitting about it, and one in particular continually poking and stirring the smouldering pile, while the others gathered more fuel and flung it on in haste. He called instantly to Pierce, Keen, and Deep, and offering them his telescope by turns, begged to know whether they agreed with him, that those Fairies were Spite, the mother of Mischief, Mischief herself, Slander, Sneer, Gossip, Idlewords, and Twaddle; and as they all cried " Yes," Farsight shut up his telescope, and said, " The awful plot is discovered! Those miscreants kindled the fire which has so shamefully blackened our merry Prince Glee, and the two lovely Maids of Honour, Clipsome and Touchy. Their object is to sow discord between Prince Glee and Princess Trill; to separate them, and destroy their happiness ! "

The Conspiracy Unveiled and

5

The Queen was instantly apprised of the detection of the infamous conspiracy, and the moment the Royal Yacht touched the shore, the four officers, with a select company of Guards, rushed along the shore to the capture of the criminals. Spite saw them coming first, and perceiving no chance of escape, she determined to rely on her sanctity and respectability; put a fair face on the matter, and walked statelily to meet them, while Mischief sat laughing and poking amongst the sticks to keep them ablaze; but Slander, Sneer, Gossip, Idlewords, and Twaddle were struck with such a panic of fear that they tried to run off and get away, but Lightfoot, Swiftfoot, and Holdfast were after them in a moment, and they were soon caught and secured. Their arms were pinioned, and their ankles strapped, so that they could only take little steps, and they were thus ignominiously led away to the Grand Justice Hall, adjoining Fairy Queen's Air Palace, in the wooded chine of the rocks. Spite, by

The Capture of the Miscreants.

reason of her boasted high birth and fine connections, was permitted to walk un-bound, with Pierce and Deep on either side and Keen behind her ; and in those circumstances she looked a very miserable little Spite, and would hardly have been known for the lean old Fairy with the fern train, and enormous long legs, who ventured to go to Elfin-Court Ball with the assumption of royal state. Farsight took charge of Mischief, who had not attempted flight, because she never cared for the conse-quences of what she had done half so much as she enjoyed doing it.

The Court assembles

When the Guards arrived with their prisoners, the Grand Hall of Justice was crowded with everybody then at Court. Fairy Queen was seated on her Golden Throne, with Prince Goldheart beside her and Judge Grim on her left hand. Prince Glee and the two Maids of Honour were ac-commodated with stools on the second step of the Daïs, and Princess Trill was supported by Mother Dignity in the background.

The seven prisoners, Spite, Mischief, Slander, Sneer, Gossip, Idlewords, and Twaddle, were ordered to mount upon the platform of Shame, that they might be seen of all the Court, and the Grand Pomp having proclaimed silence, Specs, the Public Accuser, read the indictment, which charged them with having gathered fuel, piled it up in a stack, kindled it into a blaze, and then fanned up a great fire on the shores of Sheneland, in the wicked design of blackening three of Fairy Queen's loyal subjects: to wit, Prince Glee and the fair Maids of Honour, Clipsome and Touchy. Further, the indictment charged them with an attempt to make dissension between true lovers, which attempt was the most aggravated form of High Treason recognised by the laws of Sheneland, and deserving of the punishment of *Death*.

To learn the Indictment.

Then did all the seven prisoners shake in their shoes most terribly. But they were permitted to speak in their own defence, and six of them—namely, Spite, Slander, Sneer, Gossip, Idlewords, and Twaddle, pleaded not guilty. Spite, Slander, Sneer, and Gossip contented themselves with a flat denial of the crime imputed to them ; but Idlewords rambled in her talk, and threw great discredit on their plea ; and Twaddle, who was always a weak-minded Fairy, lost herself in a maze of moral aphorisms, by means of which she contradicted herself repeatedly, and all but confessed her guilt, by admitting that she had assisted in what she then considered to be a righteous and necessary piece of work, though, now that she was made sensible of her error, she was eager to repent and amend her ways for the future. Everybody in Court laughed at Twaddle's hypocritical virtue, but when Lawyers Double and Twist cross-examined her, she fell into a terrible fright, and let them delude her into admitting herself guilty of a hundred crimes which ought in reality to have been charged on Spite and Slander.

The Coward-ice of the Guilty and

The Derision in Court.

The trial was long, careful, and extremely interesting, and the accusation was fully brought home to all the seven prisoners. All had helped to collect fuel, but it was proved that Spite had suggested the making of the fire to Mischief, and that Mischief had been afterwards the most diligent in keeping it up. The alleged spontaneous combustion was completely negatived by the finding of a flint, steel, and tinder-box in Spite's pocket. Then Mischief, perceiving that they were found out and sure to be punished, laughed, and said audaciously, " I don't care, it was very good fun while it lasted ! We *did* make the fire, and Spite played bellows, and blew it up her own self, let her deny it as long as she likes ! "

On this Spite, who had assumed an air of scornful and persecuted virtue, became aware that if she did not make a vigorous effort her newly-gained reputation for sanctity and respectability would soon be gone ; so turning upon Mischief she squeaked out indignantly, " You most

The Confession of Mischief.

THE·TRIAL·WAS
LONG, CAREFUL, &
INTERESTING

arrogant, flippant, and feeble-minded minx, how dare you support the false accusations against *me* whom *you* never saw in your life before ? "

But Mischief only laughed in her face, and Judge Grim stood up, and, in a voice that shook the Grand Justice Hall to its foundations, he pronounced the following sentences against the seven prisoners on the platform of Shame. Thus he spoke :—

ber Mockery of Aunt Spite.

" Spite, thou art the Mother of Mischief, and must suffer for the evil training thou hast given her, as well as for thy own misdeeds. Her Majesty graciously wills that the punishment of death be remitted, since the machinations of which thou wert the spring have failed to disunite the true lovers, Prince Glee and Princess Trill ; therefore, the sentence of the Court upon thee is that thy *Face be painted Black*, that all the loyal people of Sheneland may, henceforward, know thee for what thou art, and avoid thy company. Mischief will be *whipped*, for she is young, and may

The Judge's Sentence

mend. Slander will have *her tongue slit.* Sneer will have *her lips burnt.* Gossip, Idlewords, and Twaddle will have *their mouths stopped.* Justice is satisfied! Guards! remove the prisoners to the Stools of Penance. Brush, Scourge, Sword, Coal, and Tow, execute the sentence of the Court !"

And Fairy Queen having withdrawn with all the ladies of her Court, in the midst of a great clamour it was done.

Spite squeaked, Mischief shrieked, Slander yelled, and Sneer roared again ; but Gossip, Idlewords, and Twaddle maintained a most beautiful silence ; thankful, no doubt, to have escaped the severe punishment of their accomplices.

And in the evening, when the criminals had been disposed of, there was a Grand Supper, and a Ball after it, to celebrate the reconciliation of Prince Glee and Princess Trill, who sang and danced a fandango together before all the Court.

Clipsome and Touchy were also as gay

as Maids of Honour could be ; Clipsome danced with Frolic, and Touchy danced with Dump ; and Mother Dignity, who had her eye upon them throughout the evening, said they behaved beautifully : but Prim, Prude, and Demure had a long lecture before they went to bed for confabulating in corners with Wrinkle, Whisper, and Tippet—a pastime which was expressly forbidden to the Maids of Honour by the Queen herself.

Virtue re=warded and Indiscretion re=proved.

You will hear by and by what further adventures happened to Prince Glee and Princess Trill ; but first I must tell you the awful warning that befell Pickle, Prig, and Slumph, three very small Fairies who were related to Spite, and had been playfellows of Mischief, many of whose naughty ways they had learnt, much to their sorrow, as you will soon see.

THE AWFUL WARNING OF PICKLE, PRIG, & SLUMPH

THE following morning, when Fairy Queen issued forth from her bower at the east end of the Air Palace in the wooded chine of the rocks, she was observed by all the Court to be wearing a sad countenance and dark clothing. Immediately the four-and-twenty Maids of Honour and the four-and-twenty Pages looked solemn too, and the great dignitaries imitated the proper example and became as intensely grievous as Fairies without a grief could be.

Mother Dignity walked silently behind her Royal Mistress, who entered the Hall of Justice, and having seated herself upon

74

her Golden Throne, beckoned to Muffin, the Master of the Ceremonies, to approach. The official drew near with deep respect, to await her commands.

"Let all the Youth of Elfin Land be summoned, and let the Hall of Justice be cleared of all the elders," said her Majesty.

The Queen's Command.

And immediately it was done, and the seats were crowded with eager little Fairies, all wondering what fine entertainment was in store for them, and staring at the Queen on her Golden Throne, with only Mother Dignity behind her, and Muffin waiting for further orders.

Then spoke her Majesty again. "Call hither Professors Birch, Twig, Cane, and Ferule;" and those sour ushers appeared forthwith.

"Call also Professors Prize, Holiday, Treat, and Jolly," added the Queen; and those benign personages entered.

"Let the Elf Transformation appear;" and instantly, from nobody knew where, there came a tall figure all in white, carrying a wand in one hand, and a great bag in the other.

"Summon Fancy, the great Court Moralist and Story Teller;" and Fancy entered, looking clear and buoyant, and took the elevated seat which Muffin pointed out to him near the Golden Throne.

Things now began to wear a very serious aspect indeed, and many of the young Fairies who crowded the benches round the Hall of Justice felt exceedingly disappointed, because there was no mention of Fun at all, and neither Play nor Pantomime was in request. The four benign professors all had their hands in their pockets, but the four sour professors had their implements of office ready for service tightly embraced under the left arm.

"Bring in Pickle, Prig, and Slumph," said her Majesty. And those three miserable little dogs of Fairies were brought in.

Entry of Criminals.

"Set them up on the platform of Shame," was the next Royal command; and Muffin set them up one by one, and there they had

to stand and be looked at for ten minutes,
after which they were perched on a high
bench, and made to sit down.

What ugly little wretches they were!
All the youth in the Hall recognised them
as their naughtiest companions, with whom
they were constantly being forbidden to
play. Pickle looked quite scared, but
impudent too, as if he meant to brave out
whatever might happen to him ; Prig tucked
his legs under the seat and peeped about
with a cowardly dishonesty in his little
eyes ; and Slumph sat all in a heap and all
in a quake, like a mould of ill-made jelly.
When they had been thus exhibited for
some time before the gaze of the multitude,
her Majesty again spoke in the midst of the
profoundest silence.

The
Queen
speaks.

" You are all here assembled to witness
the awful warning about to be administered
to Pickle, Prig, and Slumph," said she
solemnly. " I pray you, young Fairies,
take heed lest you also come into their
miserable case. This is their crime. They

have robbed the nests of birds, they have stoned and otherwise maltreated harmless frogs, toads, and other reptiles ; they have destroyed insects, and in every way made themselves amenable to severe discipline. They will now listen to a Parable which Fancy, my Moralist, will relate, and afterwards they will be conducted to the private residence of Professor Birch, to whom I give it in charge to cure them of their infamous propensities."

Then Pickle, Prig, and Slumph, anticipating their awful fate, each put a finger in his mouth and began to cry ; but Muffin soon stopped the noise, and then Fancy, the Court Moralist and Story Teller, related the strange Parable of the " Ugliest Cat in Sheneland."

The Story Fancy told.

The Ugliest Cat in Sheneland.

" You are going to hear the story of the Ugliest Cat in Sheneland.

" It was a black cat, with spiteful yellow eyes, a mean, sharp tail, a back ridged like a saw, and a ' Miow, Mioo,' that made every other creature in Elfin Wood run into hiding as soon as they heard it. The name of this Ugly Cat was Cruel ; and he was so big and so strong, that he could catch and kill every other cat he met, besides hares, rabbits, water-rats, shrew-mice, and all kinds of birds that haunted the forest.

" His method of catching the birds was very ingenious and subtle. He would lie down on the grass under a tree, pretending to doze ; and then he would begin to sing, ' Purr, purr,' so long and loud, that the feathered things, full of curiosity, came and peeped shyly down at him through the leaves. But very few of them did it with impunity : for when the cat caught them looking, he fixed them with his great yellow eyes, until they began to tremble all over, then to turn giddy and faint, and the next minute they would drop into Cruel's jaws, as if they had been shot ; when he ate them up, quills, claws, beaks, feathers, and all.

Cruel's Under-hand Methods.

"But Cruel was not the most enviable person in Elfin Wood ; for he had one very powerful enemy named Worry, and it had been foretold to Cruel that whenever and wherever Worry met him, he must expect to receive the just punishment of his numerous crimes ; and this prophecy weighed heavily on Cruel's mind, because he was aware that he might meet Worry any day. Worry was a famous dog, Captain of Fairy Queen's Kennels, and the beginning of the enmity between him and Cruel was, that Cruel had killed many promising young members of Worry's family when they were taking morning airings, without their mothers, in the beautiful glades of Elfin Wood.

Cruel the Coward and Worry the Warrior.

"But that took place before Cruel became a cat. He was then a squat little boy, the only son of some decent poor people who kept one of the gates of Fairy Queen's Hunting Palace, in the forest ; but they were so foolishly fond of him, that they never corrected any of his naughty ways or debarred him from any amusement in which he chose to delight himself. One of his earliest pleasures was to sit on the doorstep of his father's and mother's house, and grin and make frightful faces at the neighbours' children as they went by to school, until some of them were so terrified that they ran a mile round by another way rather than pass the place where Cruel waited for them.

" There were two little ones, however, a brother and sister, named Courage and Kindness, who walked always hand in hand, and took no notice of him ; they even said openly that they were not afraid of him : he might twist his face into as many ugly shapes as he liked, but he could not harm them ; but Fairy Echo having carried this to Cruel's ears, he laughed maliciously, and cried out, ' Can't I hurt them ? I'll try, and then they'll know.'

Courage and kindness.

" So he gathered a heap of stones and kept them secret, and the next morning he hid himself behind the garden-hedge,

6

**Courage
to the
Rescue.**

and when Courage and Kindness appeared coming through the forest on their way to school, he began to pelt them until he struck Kindness on the neck, and made her cry ; but Courage immediately dashed at Cruel, and dragged him out of his hiding-place, beating him unmercifully, and then kicking him away in contempt, and Cruel, who had not expected this prompt punishment, was thankful to slink away with every bone in his body full of aches and pains.

" That lesson ought to have been enough for him, but it was not ; for though he never dared to molest Courage and Kindness, or any of their little companions again, he thought he should be quite safe and enjoy it almost as well if he might vex and torture the poor dumb creatures that traversed the forest ; and his foolish parents assured him that there was no harm in that, and, indeed, seemed to consider it a mark of a brave and bold spirit rather than otherwise. Thus upheld in his wickedness,

Cruel, though a thorough coward at heart, became more and more reckless and venturesome, until every living thing smaller than himself, and with a sense of fear, shrank from the sight of him.

"Now just at this time Dopple, a distinguished lady of the family of Worry at the Queen's Kennels, had a beautiful family of six little black puppies. They were all round, fat, sleek and shining like buttered black balls, and Dopple was exceedingly fond and proud of them ; it was quite a pleasure to see with what benevolence she permitted them to tumble and gambol about her dignified person. Worry took also an immense interest in them, and it was generally allowed in the Queen's Kennels that Dopple's children were the handsomest that had been born there for many generations. They were a high-spirited, frolicsome group of little fellows, and not always so obedient as they might have been — indeed, it was remembered after their sad disaster by

Dopple and her Children.

many of Dopple's friends, that she had said they were almost too much for her, and that her mind was filled with anxiety as to what they would turn out when Whip, the huntsman, took them in hand to train. And Dopple was much sympathised with on this account, especially by such of her acquaintance as had known what it was to bring up young families.

" Cruel had several times seen the six black puppies going out for a walk with their mother, but under those circumstances he was particularly careful not to meddle with them, for had he been so ill-advised as to attempt it, Mistress Dopple would very soon have made no bones of Master Cruel, and he knew-it. But while spying from a distance he made up his mind what he would do the first time he saw them set off for an excursion into the forest unprotected by their mother.

Cruel's Dastardly Plan.

" The opportunity he watched for happened but too soon. One hapless morning when Dopple's back was turned,

Wilful and Presto, the two sprightliest of the puppies, gambolled off and away before she knew that they were missing. The naughty little dogs were anxious to see the world by themselves, and they ran till they were out of breath and out of sight, lest their mother should discover their absence and overtake them before they could make good their escape. The first persons they met were Courage and Kindness on their way to school, and they had a capital game at play with them, and afterwards they trotted on merrily until they came to the house of Cruel's father and mother. They had never heard of Cruel in their lives, and so when they saw a little squat boy sitting on the doorstep, cooling his bowl of bread and milk, they peeped at him through the gate, wagged their stumpy tails, and said to each other how *nice* milk was when *puppies* were thirsty.

"Cruel heard the remark, and inviting them in, he persuaded them to take a lap

Puppies up to Mischief

at his breakfast, which, as it was boiling hot, scalded their tongues and made them squeal with pain. But Cruel only laughed; and the sight of their suffering set him on doing something worse. Catching Presto by the nape of his neck, he flung him up into the air and let him fall upon the stones, where he gave but one feeble moan and died. Wilful ran to his poor little brother, whining and barking, and then Cruel pelted him until he was dead too; after that he threw them over the gate into the dusty road, and there Courage and Kindness found their pretty playfellows lying when they came home from school.

Meet Death at his hands.

"'It is that wicked Cruel who has killed them,' said Kindness, weeping, as she took them up; 'dear old Dopple will be heartbroken!'

"And she carried them to the Queen's Kennels, and when Whip saw them he grieved over them, buried them, and comforted their mother; after which he cut a handsome bunch of knotty birch, and started at a great pace to the house of Cruel's father and mother, where he found Cruel just being put to bed by his foolish fond parents. The moment Cruel saw Whip approaching with that ominous bunch of knotty birch-twigs in his hand, he guessed what was going to befall him, and begged his mother to hide him in the cupboard ; but Whip was too quick for him, and before Cruel had time to howl once, the huntsman had his head under his arm, and was giving him such a trimming as the little wretch remembered dolorously whenever he sat down on the doorstep to eat his breakfast, for more than a month after. And during that space of time he behaved rather better, but as soon as he had forgotten the smart, he said he didn't care, and that he would serve exactly in the same way as he had served Presto and Wilful, all Dopple's other children if they fell in his way. And he did ; one after another, he succeeded in

his Well= deserved punish= ment.

killing all Dopple's six beautiful puppies, and the whole kennel went into mourning for them.

"Then Worry showed his teeth and growled out threats of deadly vengeance; and after reflecting and consulting about it for some time, Dopple and he set off to find the famous Elf Transformation; having discovered her abode they laid their piteous case before her, and asked what she could do to help them.

Elf
Trans=
forma=
tion's
Sug=
gestion

"'I can change Cruel into the Ugliest Cat in all Sheneland,' replied she.

"'That is excellent!' growled Worry. 'Change Cruel into the Ugliest Cat in all Sheneland, and the first time I see him, I'll kill him!'

"And Dopple and Worry ran home to their kennel very well contented.

The next day, Elf Transformation came down to Elfin Wood, to the house where Cruel's father and mother lived, and there sat Cruel on the doorstep, cooling his bowl of bread and milk, and waiting, as usual,

HE·BECAME·THE ❧❧
UGLIEST·CAT·IN·ALL
SHENELAND ❧ ❧ ❧

until something came by that he could hurt. Elf Transformation drew quite near and looked at him sharply ; then, making the complimentary remark that he could not well be more frightful than he was, she twitched out a tuft of his red hair, and immediately he became the Ugliest Cat in all Sheneland!

Is carried out.

" When his parents returned home, after their day's work, Cruel was still sitting on the doorstep ; but he was now washing his face with his paw, and, of course, they did not know him for their son ; but they hated cats, particularly ugly cats, so they drove him away with many kicks and hard blows ; and even his mother threw a broom after him, to frighten him farther off. So he was obliged to become a wild cat in Elfin Wood, where he was day and night exposed to be caught in traps, to be shot by Whip, or to be devoured by Worry and his friends. For ever so long, however, he contrived to exist, though very miserably ; but, at the same time, he was the terror of the forest by reason of his thefts and murders.

"There was a world of talk about him in the Queen's Kennels every evening after supper, and, at last, a grand hunting match was arranged by the whole pack, to take place on a particular day, when a handsome reward was to be given to any dog who would catch and kill Cruel. Worry licked his chaps, and said the reward was as good as in his dish already ; and bade Dopple make her mind easy, for he would never come back to kennel again while there was as much fluff left of Cruel as would stuff a bee's pillow.

"And the great day of the Hunt arrived, but it had been kept so snug, that Cruel had not heard a single whisper of it. He was sunning himself in a soft mossy nook, and digesting a full breakfast of young rabbits, when all at once he heard a horn sound, then the cry of the dogs, and the patter, patter, patter of their feet in the glade, coming up very fast indeed. He

The hunt for Cruel.

was awake in an instant, and scouring away like the wind, his mean tail brandished spike-wise, and his fur standing on end all over him ; but Worry was on his scent, and though he had a good start, Cruel lost ground at every stride, and finally was brought to bay on a space where there was no tree for him to run up ; and though he hissed, and swore, and spit, and used both claws and teeth, Worry gripped him by the back and shook the life out of him in no time.

Capture and his End.

" Then the other dogs ate him up, all but two hairs of his whiskers, and a bit of fluff, which Worry carried home to Dopple, as an assurance that her children's destroyer was no more.

" And that was the deserved end of Cruel, the Ugliest Cat in all Sheneland."

As soon as Fancy, the Court Moralist and Story Teller, had finished his Parable, the Hall of Justice rang from one end to the other with the clapping of little fairy

The Fate of the Wicked little Fairies.

hands, and cries of " Serve him right ! Serve him right ! " And as soon as the clamour had subsided, Pickle, Prig, and Slumph were delivered over into the custody of Professor Birch, who immediately conducted them to his private residence and initiated them into the mysteries of his discipline, by which cruelty, craft, and insensibility were gradually eradicated from the fairy temper.

When they had disappeared, Muffin, by the Queen's command, dismissed the assemblage to play, and to partake of a refection in the open air, after which the young Fairies returned home, powerfully edified and impressed by all they had seen and heard.

THE REWARD of COURAGE & KINDNESS

AIRY QUEEN was even more ready to give treats to good little Fairies, than she was to grant proper correction to naughty little Fairies; so the day after the Awful Warning of Pickle, Prig, and Slumph, she consulted with Mother Dignity and Muffin, Master of the Ceremonies, as to what entertainment should be provided for Courage and Kindness and their favourite companions.

Mother Dignity suggested that they should go to bed an hour earlier than usual by way of treat ; and Muffin said, would

93

it please them, did her Majesty think, to perform double dues of lessons ? Her Majesty thought *not*, and called Fancy, the Court Moralist and Story Teller, into counsel.

Fancy would have been glad to give his Royal Mistress's little guests a new Pantomime, but as they were going to receive a public reward, he was of opinion that something more solid and improving should be set before them. What did her Majesty think of having Tuflongbo, the great Traveller of Sheneland, up to Court, to relate his wonderful adventures in the country of the Aplepivi ?

Receive their Reward.

Fancy's suggestion was excellent—was everything that could be desired ! Tuflongbo would be a capital treat, no doubt !

Now, when Tuflongbo had returned to Elfin Court, after his remarkable discoveries in the country of the Aplepivi, he had been welcomed with a complete ovation. His Royal Mistress immediately appointed him State Geographer and Astronomer, and conferred upon him the dignified order of Complacency, and the Grand Cross of Vanity, which were the two highest and pleasantest distinctions that she had it in her power to bestow. Also, she was graciously pleased to promise him that she would soon name a day when he might recite his marvellous adventures before herself and all Elfin Court, in full state assembled ; so when Fancy suggested that the good little people would like to hear him also, the Grand Pomp was immediately ordered to proclaim the entertainment with the sound of trumpets, as one that would combine valuable instruction with much amusement.

Tuf= longbo is coming !

When the appointed time arrived, the State Hall of the Air Palace was brilliantly lighted up, and in a few minutes after the doors were opened it was crowded in every part except on the Daïs, which was reserved for the Queen and the Court, and a select number of little Fairies especially pointed out by Professor Prize as worthy of that honourable distinction. A small elevated pulpit was reserved for Tuflongbo, and a little gallery in the roof was appropriated to the Royal Society of Wiseacres of Sheneland, most of whom had combined, through envy and jealousy of the honours paid him, not to believe a word Tuflongbo might say, even before he opened his mouth. Tippet and Wink had made interest to be received amongst this choice knot of bright and amiable spirits, and as soon as Tuflongbo appeared on the platform, smirking and bowing to Fairy Queen and the Court right and left, Tippet could not forbear whispering that the fellow was a conceited, fantastical idiot ; in which remarkable expression of opinion most of the Royal Society of Wiseacres cordially acquiesced.

The Arrival of the great Travel= let.

Tuflongbo was a little, wiry, brown fellow with no hair on his head but a great deal on his chin. His countenance showed that internally he was fortified with much buckram, and his dress was as striking as it was possible to be ; but then he had had surprising adventures, and therefore could claim a right to be distinguished by the vulgar eye as well as by the discerning mind ; and if he had not worn a cloak of peacocks' eyes who would have known him at a glance, as they did now, to be the celebrated person he was ? He wore over the cloak the ribbon of the Order of Complacency, and the Grand Cross of Vanity decorated his breast.

Fairy Queen being comfortably settled, with Mother Dignity and her Maids of Honour grouped around her, Muffin gave the Signal of Attention, and Tuflongbo immediately opened his narrative as follows, dispensing with all nervousness and all circumlocution :—

He commences his Story.

The Adventures of Tuflongbo, related by Himself.

"When your Fairy Majesty last graciously

7

gave me leave of absence from Elfin Court, you were pleased to express a desire to learn what became of the Old Moons when they disappeared from our firmament. Your Majesty's curiosity was most laudable, and also most gratifying to me as a fervent disciple of science. Previous astronomers have made diligent inquiries in that direction, but I need hardly say with what a total failure of success. The honour and glory of solving this important problem, and making an immortal discovery, was reserved for ME ! "

And then Tuflongbo drew himself up, expanded his little chest, and glanced triumphantly at the Royal Society of Wiseacres in the Gallery.

" It was reserved for ME," he repeated, " to add another and a glorious chapter to the annals of Fairy Science, and to bring this tremendous and ancient mystery to a safe and unimpeachable solution. It is extremely gratifying to me, after my many perils, to lay such a precious page of knowledge before the assembled beauty, wit, learning, and youth of Sheneland, and especially before your Majesty, to whose service it is equally my pride and my pleasure to dedicate every waking moment of my existence." (Loud applause.)

"Perhaps your Majesty may graciously be pleased to remember that when I set out on my last journey of exploration I took the South road through Sheneland, intending to pass by the Country of the Gnomes, who work in the Mines, but I was diverted from my original intention by an unforeseen accident ; and leaving that route, I turned off to the West, and travelled onward until I came to World's End, which is bounded by a lofty wall of stone and bricks. When I saw this obstacle my heart almost failed me (so short-sighted are we), though at that very moment I was on the verge of my great discovery, and at the dawn of the proudest day of my life !" (Great applause.)

His Miraculous Journey and

"Over this wall there grew a stout

trailing plant, with a five-peaked glossy leaf, and clusters of dark purple berries; and up this I climbed arduously until I had gained the summit, and through tears of joy beheld the wonders of the strange country beyond. As my vision cleared, imagine my ecstasy—imagine my overwhelming delight at discerning in the plain immediately below me a vast body of men in blue aprons, cutting up the Old Moons and making Stars of them!"

Here Tuflongbo paused, utterly overcome by his recollections, and the tremendous applause that ensued lasted several minutes, interspersed with ironical cheers from the Wiseacres' Gallery. Tuflongbo bowed to them with his hand on his heart, and when the tumult subsided he continued his narrative.

His Wonderful Discovery.

"The joy of this discovery was greater than words can express. Here was a question, which had agitated scientific circles for years, set at rest for ever! Here was a convincing proof of the Universal Economy of Nature! What a beautiful simplicity is there in the explanation of this antique puzzle! A band of men in blue aprons cutting up the Old Moons and making Stars of them! I was so lost in wonder and admiration that I remained for some hours spellbound, and watching the process of conversion undiscovered; but at length the Chief Polisher threw back his head, opened his mouth in a wide yawn, and I caught his eye. The only course left for me to pursue was to bow and introduce myself, which civility he received with the utmost politeness; and after presenting my credentials as the State Traveller of Sheneland, he became still more courteous, and invited me to make a stay at his house, but I excused myself as having further discoveries to make, and a long journey still before me." (Applause.)

The Making of the Stars.

" This highly satisfactory commencement to my travels filled me with new courage to encounter my difficulties, and I made great and rapid progress, until one evening when I arrived on the shores of a vast sea, quite unknown to geographers, and upon which no sail was discernible. My heart sank before this emergency. I paced the shore for hours, cogitating on the apparent impossibility of traversing this immense body of water; but at length I was relieved by seeing approach a tall old man with a bundle of nets in his arms. I began to question him concerning the navigation of this strange sea; its tides, reefs, shoals, and opposite shores. He did not seem to understand any inquiry but the last, and to that he replied, that if I crossed the sea I should be immediately in the Country of the Aplepivi." (Applause.)

Tuf= longbo in Difficul= ties.

" ' But how cross it ? ' I asked him.

" ' Easily. It is but three sights over,' he replied emphatically.

" ' *But three sights over* ' ? I repeated. ' Will you be pleased to explain the meaning of that expression ! '

" ' It is only this :—Stand on the shore,

look to the horizon, and jump—that is *one* sight. Pause, look, and jump again—that is *two* sights. Pause, look, and jump again—that is *three* sights. And behold you landed in the Country of the Aplepivi ! '

" ' But how about *sinking* ? ' I suggested.

" ' The water is so buoyant that a little fellow like you cannot sink,' was his assurance.

" ' *Little fellow !* there you have hit another of my difficulties,' said I. ' How can I jump as far as I can see ? I can see a thousand miles at least.'

" ' Nothing simpler. Watch me, and instantly you will be able to do it. I will go across to the Country of the Aplepivi and back again in the twinkling of an eyelash.'

" So said, so done ! Without further preface he leaped to the horizon ; the second spring carried him out of sight ; but before I had time to cry ' How marvellous ! ' he was again standing beside me, perfectly cool and unfatigued. I then shook hands

3s sbown bow to over= come tbem.

with him, thanked him for his courteous instructions, and took my spring success-**One, two, three, and away! to**fully,—once, twice, thrice, and found myself safely landed on the snow-white shores of the Country of the Aplepivi ! "

At this point of Tuflongbo's narrative the applause became tumultuous, and the Royal Society of Wiseacres in the Gallery were reduced to a most crestfallen silence, while a little boy from the Country under the Sun, who was stated to be on a visit to Professor Holiday, shouted tremendously —" My stars ! but that beats the Electric Telegraph hollow ! "

Tuflongbo refreshed himself with a sip of negus, and after a short pause resumed the story of his great adventures.

" Yes—those three remarkable springs landed me sound in wind and limb on the snow-white shores of the Country of the **The Aplepivi Country.** Aplepivi, into which, before me, no traveller had ever gained admittance. My first impression of it was that there was a great dearth of inhabitants ; but, in fact, the

Aplepivi had received warning of the coming of a powerful and distinguished stranger, and had retreated to their fortified towns and villages, leaving the open country quite deserted. I therefore had an opportunity of making my earliest researches without impediment ; and first I took notice of a beautiful tree, on the singular fruit of which I supped delightfully.

" This fruit was large and oval in shape, the exterior of it being a crisp and delicate brown, light as puff. On breaking through this crust I found the interior to be a luscious, sweet, juicy compound, most acceptable to the palate, and most fragrant to the organs of smell. This fruit grew in handsome clusters of four at the end of each branch, and some trees I observed to be so heavily laden with it as to be almost bent to the ground. I afterwards learnt that it formed the staple food of the Aplepivi, and I have since been led into a conjecture that their name may be derived from the name of this fruit ; but this is

Tuflong-bo tastes its Luscious Fruit.

rather a question for Philologists than for your Gracious Majesty's State Geographer and Astronomer."

This part of Tuflongbo's narrative had been received by Fairy Queen, by all the Court, by all the little Fairies, by the boy from the Country under the Sun, who was staying with Professor Holiday, and even by the Wiseacres' Gallery, with the profoundest silence and the deepest interest ; and when the great traveller paused to refresh himself with another sip of negus, a discussion arose as to the practicability of naturalising this charming fruit of the Aplepivi in Sheneland. Her Majesty deigned to consult Tuflongbo herself, and everybody was thrown into ecstasy when he replied that he had foreseen his Royal Mistress's wish, and had brought home abundance of cuttings of the wonderful tree ; and not only cuttings, but a hamper of the finest and best-ripened fruits, upon which he had the honour of inviting her Majesty, with all her Court and the youthful members

his Fore= thought.

of his audience, to sup, after he had finished the recital of all his most remarkable adventures and discoveries. He then went on, his hearers being in the highest good-humour at the prospect of such an excellent supper ; and Muffin, Master of the Cere-monies, stole slyly out to put the clock on.

" After I had eaten of this refreshing fruit," Tuflongbo proceeded, " a drowsiness overcame me, and lying down under the tree from whose branches I had plucked it, I enjoyed a long and refreshing slumber. I slept until the morning, and then rose, determined at once vigorously to pursue my researches into the ways and customs of the singular tribe of the Aplepivi. And first I took my note- and sketch-books,— which I shall have the greatest pride and pleasure in submitting to your Majesty at a convenient time,—and, pencil in hand, I proceeded to thread my way through mazy and fruitful groves until I came suddenly upon a cluster of circular straw huts, from which issued swarms upon

Naughty
Old
Muffin!

swarms of the Aplepivi, all humming and buzzing incoherently. They were a little and insignificant people to behold, but they were blessed with a vast sense of their own importance, and I was advised to maintain a respectful distance between myself and their dwellings, lest I should give offence and draw upon me their wrath if I approached inquisitively near. My arrival was plainly regarded as an intrusion, but as it behoved me to secure their goodwill, or to fail in the chief objects of my mission, I drew softly near, extending towards them a branch covered with large white blossoms, in token of amity. After a few moments of hesitation and discussion some of the chief Aplepivi flew upon the branch and thrust their round little brown heads into the cups of the flowers ; after which the buzz of anger subsided, and they opened the conversation in the most friendly manner.

The Inhabit= ants of Aplepivi

" I now discovered that this singular people wore little wings under their shoulders, and presently I added to my stock of knowledge the fact that they were furnished with a deadly weapon with which they promptly avenged every insult, and, on occasion, executed unanimously any obnoxious member of their own tribes who had degraded himself by losing or making away with his weapon. I found amongst them later many admirable customs worthy of being introduced into Sheneland, and came to the final conclusion that they were a people to be respected, and one with whom our nation might advantageously form alliances.

And their habits.

" When, therefore, a Chief Senator of the tribe inquired of me : ' What brings the great Traveller Tuflongbo into the humble country of the Aplepivi ?' I answered, ' The pursuit of knowledge, and the desire to extend our commerce,' being ever eager to extend your Majesty's influence in foreign lands. But my last remark was met with some indignation.

" ' The Aplepivi do not engage in commerce, they are an aristocratic people,' said the Chief Senator, with a great hauteur. 'They are also warlike and wealthy, and they have quite enough to do to protect the rich stores they possess against being pillaged by bands of robbers from the Country under the Sun, who come periodically into our towns and villages with a great brazen sound of instruments which stuns us into helplessness ; while we are in that state they rifle our dwellings, and leave them as bare as a field over which a flight of locusts has passed. Never have we formed any treaty yet which has not turned ultimately to our loss and disadvantage.'

" He then flew away, and I began to fear my embassy would come to nought, when a shrewd and experienced councillor, who had listened and reflected while the Senator addressed me, now spoke and said—

The Conference

" ' Let us hear a little more about it, Tuflongbo. What can you Sheneland folk give the Aplepivi in return for fruit, and

What
can you
give the
Aple-
pivi?

for their housed store which is golden honey ? '

" ' We can give you plains of purple heather, and fields of bean-blossom,' I replied. ' Send over a colony of your people to behold the fertility of our land : only give me now certain specimens of your products to take to Fairy Queen at Elfin Court, and I will use my best persuasions to gain for them permission to settle on the Downs of Sheneland, when they can pay tribute in kind.'

" And immediately the great Parliament of the Aplepivi was convened to take the matter into consideration, and after such a buzzing as drowned my voice completely, it was agreed that I should receive one hundred and twenty pots of the finest honey, and twelve score hampers of fruit of Aplepivi, all of which await your Majesty, the Court, and the little people on the supper-table at this moment ; for I perceive that the clock is on the stroke of nine, and that Muffin has yawned

And its
Lucky
Issue.

thrice as a sign that there has been talk enough."

Muffin, in fact, had put the clock on an hour.

And so Tuflongbo, who was a fellow of infinite tact, brought his narrative to a close, and everybody went in to supper except the occupants of the Wiseacres' Gallery, who were not invited. They hovered about the Court, and tried to persuade each other that there was nothing but bubbles in all Tuflongbo had said ; but when they saw dish after dish of the wonderful fruit of the Aplepivi carried into the supper-hall, and pot after pot of honey, with new bread and bowls of cream, their appetites became keen, and they wished that if they *were* bubbles, they had the chance of trying the flavour of them.

At last they grew so hungry that they got all about the door, peeping in at the crevices and keyhole, and once, when it was opened to call for more honey, and more

Hurrah for Supper!

cream, and more new bread, and more fruit of Aplepivi, one of the fattest of the Wise-acres fell in with a crash ; and Tuflongbo, who was a good-natured fellow in the main, looking round, saw all the clever hungry faces and invited them in to supper. And everybody had as much as he could eat, both of honey and fruit of Aplepivi, and new bread and delicious cream, and Tuflongbo became from that time forth one of the most popular Fairies in Sheneland.

Moreover, the Great Court Doctor Pille stated as his professional opinion that the new fruit and the golden honey which Tuflongbo had introduced into Sheneland were wholesome articles of food, especially for the younger Fairies; and that he recommended the wonderful fruit of the Aplepivi to be served at least twice a week in the season, as a relief to rice pudding, sago, and tapioca, which had hitherto been the monotonous traditions of every nursery. He said also that bread-and-honey were

Dr. Pille becomes popular.

8

good for the little people at any time of the day when they felt hungry.

After supper it was proposed, put to the vote, and passed unanimously, that, as a mark of admiration and respect, a statue in Puff Paste should be erected to Tuflongbo near the Sun Pavilion, in commemoration of his discovery of the use to which the Old Moons are put, and of the introduction into Sheneland of Golden Honey and Fruit of Aplepivi.

And the next day the Queen signed a commission, and Tuflongbo again set off on his important travels with a view to discovering the whereabouts of the Puff-raspabi and the Alicompagni, two lost tribes which emigrated from Sheneland during the heavy reign of Queen Dull, and whom it was considered by Prince Goldheart highly desirable to recall. And Tuflongbo had everybody's best wishes for his success in his carpet-bag when he set off.

Good=
bye,
Tuf=
longbo!

THE CONSPIRACY of SPITE
& THE MASKSELLERS

YOU have not forgotten the signal punishment of Spite and her accomplices, for engaging in a plot to separate Prince Glee and Princess Trill ? We must now return to them.

When Spite had been painted black she looked particularly hideous, but she bore herself loftily, notwithstanding, and declared that her face was as white as anybody's. Her acquaintance was now, of course, always disowned in public, but she still had her friends in private ; and when the blackest black wore off her features she went into society again for a little while much as usual ; but being discountenanced by all persons of station, and placed under the surveillance of Spy, she thought it as well to retire to Castle Craft, whence she could carry on a correspondence with her friends at Court with less annoyance to herself.

Spite and her Friends appear once more,

Her companions in guilt and punishment were also soon in high feather again ; for though Slander now stammered, and Sneer laughed on the wrong side of her mouth, and though Gossip, Idlewords, and Twaddle spoke through their noses, they pretended to have quite forgotten their experiences on the Stools of Penance, and vowed they had never been in disgrace at all. Indeed, nobody but the lawyers and jailers would ever have suspected how often they got into trouble ; for they had made the acquaintance of Specious, Plausible, and False Pretences, who had set up as Masksellers in Sheneland, and whenever they were caught they puzzled Judge Grim,

and Specs, the Public Accuser, by wearing
a new mask on an old face.

Fairy Queen and Prince Goldheart would
gladly have banished from Sheneland both
the Mask-sellers and all those who resorted
to them ; but by certain laws, made during
the bad reign of Queen Dull, their trade
was protected as well as their persons ;
and so there they remained, and, with
Mischief ever ready to lend them a helping
hand, they succeeded in making many
Fairies truly miserable, notwithstanding the
wise and merciful government of Fairy
Queen and Prince Goldheart.

Now Spite, shut up in her country
residence of Castle Craft, had not thought
it needful to apply to the Mask-sellers on
her own account ; but one day, her friend
and correspondent, Wrinkle, wrote to her
that she had been to see Specious, and had
got him to paint her a new face, which
made her look quite young again by moon-
light. She added, further, that if Spite had
a mind to come up to Court for the grand

Ready
for any
Wicked=
ness.

entertainments which were soon to take place, no doubt Specious would be able to fit her out so as to defy even the recognition of Spy.

Now Spite, old as she was, loved gaiety to such an excess that the thought of Grand Entertainments at Elfin Court without the light of her presence, gave her the most acute pain. All that day, after receiving Wrinkle's letter, she sat by herself, biting her nails and wondering what great event was to be celebrated by the entertainments. At last she grew tired of speculating, and determined to write to Gossip for all the news that she could collect. Gossip had not much to do

Spite's Visitor

when she got Spite's communication, or, at least, what she had to do could wait awhile ; so she set off to Castle Craft in person, as the bearer of her own intelligence, and arrived just at nightfall.

Spite welcomed her with much satisfaction, and when they grew cosy at supper their talk became quite confidential.

"Now, dear Gossip, I am almost dying of curiosity, do begin and tell me what is going to happen at Court," said Spite, with wily affection.

"Make up your mind to something that will vex you *extremely*," replied Gossip, shaking her head significantly.

"What is it?" asked Spite, aghast.

"*Prince Glee and Princess Trill are going to be married*," said Gossip.

"Going to be married! Without asking my consent? Impossible! It can never be! It *shall* never be!" By the time Spite had uttered these vehement exclamations she was scarlet in the face, and shaking all over with passion. Gossip went on eating quite coolly.

"All Sheneland is talking about it, Spite; *all Sheneland*, I assure you," she said, popping a bit of pie into her mouth. "It will be such a wedding as has not taken place at Elfin Court in this generation. Fairy Queen herself will give the Princess a dower, and it is rumoured that Prince

Tells her News of

Glee will get the appointment of Master of the Revels at the Isle of Palms. Old Woman, who lives in the hollow of the Ash-Tree, is spinning gossamer night and day as fast as she can spin, and her little Maid Brisk is on foot from dusk to dawn gathering silver rays, and from dawn to dusk gathering dewsprent webs and silk of flowers. No expense will be spared to make everything worthy of the event and of the chief actors in it. Already the Royal Cooks are at work, and the orders that have been sent out for fruit of Aplepivi, for honey, for custard and cream-tarts, for nectar of clover, and all manner of delicious dainties, is beyond belief! The day *before* the wedding there is to be a Picnic in Elfin Wood, with music and dancing on the greensward, and in the evening a pantomime and a state supper. *After* the wedding there will be a Ball, surpassing even that at which Prince Glee and Princess Trill appeared when the Prince had stolen the Princess

The Wedding Preparations.

Maid
Brisk
gathering
Rays off
the Wild
White
Roses.

away from this very agreeable country residence. I have got cards for everything, and as you are not likely to see the fine doings yourself, I'll come down here again and tell you all about them when they are over."

"Thank you for *nothing*, Gossip," hissed Spite, grinning frightfully in her friend's face; "but I mean to be there myself; *and there'll be no wedding*, I can tell you that; *there'll be no wedding!*"

"You need not look so ugly, Aunt Spite; I don't care whether there is or not! When you get into a passion, your face is as black as if Brush had only just operated upon it!" said Gossip in a pet.

"And you need not snuffle and talk through your nose so much," retorted Spite, "as if Tow had only just stopped your mouth!"

"You are very uncivil, Aunt Spite; and I shall leave you to get the rest of the news how and where you can!" cried Gossip.

Spite's Prophecy

" You have told me all I want to know, and so now be off with you, and a good riddance of bad rubbish ! " shrieked Spite.

And so Gossip departed from Castle Craft, and being returned to Elfin Court, she made everybody laugh by detailing the particulars of her visit, and repeating how Spite had threatened that *there should be no wedding.* Spy heard of what Spite had said, and immediately he and Watch were on the alert, lest she should creep up to Court in disguise, and really attempt some mischief to Prince Glee or Princess Trill.

Fairy Queen, Prince Goldheart, and the Prince and Princess were also informed of the malicious old creature's threat, but they did not feel it of sufficient importance to make them uneasy, and the preparations for the wedding went on without check or hindrance.

But, nevertheless, Spite outwitted them all, and came up to Court as a Stranger from the Country, and even Spy did not know her. How she was enabled to do so you are now going to learn.

When Gossip left Castle Craft, Spite took some time to cool down and recover herself; but presently she said, "Wrinkle's suggestion is the best. I'll go to the Mask-sellers' and buy a new face, and then we shall see what we shall see, my pretty Trill. You'll be a bird singing in a cage before long, I promise you; and Prince Glee may peck at the bars till he's a hundred, but he'll never get you out!"

And so Spite put on her cloak, pulled her hood over her head, took her staff in her hand, and telling young Fibs, the secret doorkeeper of Castle Craft, that he might expect her back every minute until he saw her, she set out on her journey to the Chief City of Sheneland, where lived Specious, Plausible, and False-Pretences. As it was Specious who had been so successful in making Wrinkle look young again, Spite determined to consult with him first; and it was very lucky for her she did; for

She starts on her Journey

when she reached his dwelling, which was situated in one of the narrowest and dismallest back-streets, she found that he was giving a tea-party to his friends, amongst whom she found Plausible and False-Pretences, and her own old cronies, Slander, Whisper, and Sneer.

The meeting was delightful to all; Slander, Whisper, and Sneer said they were charmed to see their dear friend Spite once more ; and Spite declared herself thankful to meet them again, too ; for, said she, with a profound sigh, " I have no congenial society within reach of Castle Craft, and never see a civilised creature to speak to from one week's end to another, unless poor Malice drops in to pay me a morning visit."

And meets some Old Acquaintances.

So all her friends condoled with Spite, and Whisper said she must come back to Elfin Court by hook or by crook, for Castle Craft was no sphere for her talents ; and Spite said in her ear confidentially that what Whisper suggested was the object of

her present visit to the Mask-sellers'. In
a few moments all the company round the
tea-table had been slyly informed of Spite's
business, and when the urn had been
carried out, a dark lantern was put in its
place, the tray and empty trenchers were
removed, and Specious brought forth his
books of disguises of every pattern that
the ingenuity of Old Lies, False, and Crafty
had ever been able to invent.

Slander, Sneer, and Whisper began to
turn them over with much stealthy enjoyment, and to mention which they should
like best to wear if they had a plot in hand ;
but Spite was more attracted by the singular
masks hanging on the walls, for she had
lived long enough to learn that it is by
countenance, and not by clothes, that
wise folks judge, and that Spite in gossamer
of gold would be Spite still, as plainly as if
she went up to Court in her penitential
robes, and with her visage as black as
Brush painted it.

Choosing
the
Mask.

Specious walked round the room with

her, talking low, and pointing out the various merits of his masks ; Plausible and False-Pretences listened, and now and then put in a word of advice ; and Spite began to feel that the way to Court was becoming exceedingly smooth before her. By degrees she let out to the three Mask-sellers that she wished to prevent the Marriage of Prince Glee and Princess Trill above all things, and that at any price it *must* be accomplished. Specious, Plausible, and False - Pretences immediately drew together, and consulted about the means, while Spite waited anxiously to hear what they made out. False-Pretences observed that she showed a marked admiration for a very sleek, oily mask with fixed creases of smiles about the mouth, and a languishing, watery look in the eyes, and this gave him an idea.

A Villain= ous Plot

"I have it!" cried he unctuously ; "we will first make a mask exactly like our friend Spite here, and fit it with straps ; then we will make another mask on the model of Pious Hypocrisy, which she shall put on. It passes with favour in almost every form of society, and thus disguised, our excellent client will be able to return to Elfin Court without exciting the smallest suspicion. She will carry under her cloak the copy of her own face ; and having gained admittance into Princess Trill's bower, she will beguile her with crafty conversation, gently slip the mask from its concealment, put it on the Princess, and strap it fast under her flowing golden hair."

"What a triumphant device ! " cried Specious and Plausible simultaneously ; but Spite, though pleased, was cautious, and wished to know what next.

"What next ? " echoed False-Pretences. "Everything you like next. From the moment that the mask imitated from your own face is put on Princess Trill, all her friends will avoid her. Prince Glee himself will not know her ; Fairy Queen will forbid her the Court ; the Maids of Honour will ridicule her ; Wink will play her tricks ;

Hatched by False-Pretences.

and she will be brought to the very verge of despair."

"And at that moment," said Plausible, taking up the word as his fellow mask-seller dropped it, "you, in your new character, will drop in with oily consolations ; you will beguile her away from the precincts of the Palace, draw her deep into Elfin Wood, and then she will be in your power, and you can carry her off to Castle Craft, or to any other safe place of captivity which you may prefer."

"I shall not take her to Castle Craft again," said Spite. "No, no ; I'll make her trip farther than Castle Craft, I promise her."

"Where will you take her, dear Spite ? " asked Whisper insinuatingly.

Whisper is curious.

"I shall not tell you," retorted Spite. "So if you think to get some fun yourself by setting Prince Glee on her track, you'll be disappointed ; and if he is silly enough to go in search of her again, a pretty wild-goose chase I'll give him, you may rely on it."

" Come, come, ladies, no quarrelling ;
let all go softly," said Plausible ; " we have
not finished our business yet. There are
the masks to make ; and I want to know
if there is any chance of getting Elf Transformation on our side."

" Not the smallest chance in the world,"
replied Spite. " Elf Transformation always
holds with those detestable relatives of
mine, Justice and Truth."

" We should do almost as well, if we
could get possession of her wand," observed
Specious.

" If little Prig were free, I daresay he
would have stolen it for us ; but Professor
Birch has got hold of him," answered
Spite.

" Then we must manage without it—
at anyrate, Mischief is always at your
beck and call."

" Oh yes ! And I am a person of many
devices myself. Only let me get within
reach of Princess Trill, and she will not
escape me."

9

"Then we will summon the craftsmen, and get the Masks made at once," said Specious.

"Do, by all means, and I shall reach Elfin Court to-night: I shall go to the Picnic, and dance on the sward."

"Stop, madam!" cried False-Pretences, in alarm; "you must act up to your character. *Pious Hypocrisy does not go to picnics, and does not dance on the sward.* If you would gratify your passion of spite against Prince Glee and Princess Trill, you must forego every other indulgence until that is accomplished."

The Making of the Mask, and

Spite sulkily acquiesced in the propriety of this; and having taken her seat in the operating chair, Waxy was called, and made a model from her face, while Guile and Smirk copied the Mask of Pious Hypocrisy, which she was to wear over her own dark and sharp features. Waxy's model was admitted by everybody to be perfection; and when Daub had coloured it, Whisper said in the ear of her tart friend,

" Now, my dear, you see yourself as others see you ; " and giggled with glee at Spite's vexation. Spite, however, put up with the insolence, and pretended not to notice Sneer's significant expression, for she had no wish to alienate her acquaintance at present ; and when the Mask of Pious Hypocrisy was finished, she put it on, drew her hood up over her head, and smiled upon them, quite another person.

" Well, I declare ! " cried Whisper, under her breath.

Its great Success.

" I should never have known her ! " said Slander ; but Sneer looked very much as if she discerned something of her old friend still under all that mask of oily blandness.

" I think our plot may be pronounced a success," remarked Plausible, rubbing his grisly hands ; and both Specious and False-Pretences agreed with him, and were full of admiration at the artist-like work of Guile and Smirk.

" I shall only wear my mask so long as it serves my purpose, for it will be very irksome," said Spite uneasily; "you will receive it back by the hand of Mischief as soon as ever I have got clear away from Elfin Court with Princess Trill."

"Keep it by you, you may need it again," exclaimed Specious. "We have made you a conspiracy, and furnished you with means to carry it on, but we never answer for success if our rules and counsels are neglected."

"Stuff and nonsense!" retorted Spite; "you are a pack of knaves, and——"

"Madam, I *implore* you, *speak in character*, or all is lost!" cried Plausible, going down on his knees to her.

"Fudge! Well, my beloved friends, I beg to take a grateful leave of you, to thank you for your amiable hospitality, and courteously to bid you remember me in your orisons. Fare ye well, fare ye well!"

The Commencement of the Journey.

And, with a creasy smile on her broad new face, Spite left the Mask-sellers' dwelling, and set out on her journey to Elfin Court.

WHO·ARE·YOU·THAT·
MOLEST·PEACEABLE·
WAYFARERS? ✒ ✒ ✒

SPITE'S JOURNEY TO ELFIN COURT

IT was quite dark when Spite set off on her journey; and she had not gone far when she set her foot on something soft, and jumped aside with a scream as she heard some creature giggling up overhead amongst the branches of the trees.

"Who are you that molest peaceable wayfarers?" said she, in a voice to match her Mask of Pious Hypocrisy.

"I am the Wicked Fairy of the Creeping Plant with many Tendrils, old Friend," replied the giggling, ape-like creature, grinning down on her.

The
Wicked
Fairy's
recogni=
tion of
Spite.

"*Old Friend, indeed!* I don't know

133

you ; and I'll trouble you not to claim the acquaintance of respectable people ! " cried Spite, in a rage.

At this the Wicked Fairy of the Creeping Plant with many Tendrils giggled all the more ; and when he had done giggling, he hissed out, " I can see in the dark, and *I know you, Aunt Spite,* for all you have been to the Mask-sellers' and got fitted out so prettily."

" Hush ! not a word, *Friend,*" now whispered Spite, quaking from head to foot. " You won't betray me, *Friend* ? "

bis Wel= come Gift.

" Not I ; go, and take my good wishes with you, and these tendrils, for you may have a use for them ; " and with that he threw her down a bundle as strong as cords, which she picked up and put in her pocket.

As she again moved to go on, she trod on the soft thing once more ; it lurched and groaned, and Spite, with another start and jump, asked angrily, " Who have you got tied down here, amongst the nettles ? "

" It is little Idle, who was Old Woman's

Maid," replied the Wicked Fairy up in the tree.

" Oh, by the bye, where does Old Woman live ? I want to make inquiry of her concerning the festivities that are soon to take place at Elfin Court," said Spite. " I daresay she will know everything, as she is the chief gossamer weaver."

" She lives in the Hollow of the Ash-Tree, about half a mile off, on the left-hand side as you go," answered the Wicked Fairy of the Creeping Plant with many Tendrils. " She will tell you all you wish to know, **Off to Old Woman's.** for Gossip has just left her ; and her little Maid, Brisk, will set out to gather rays and silver stripes as soon as ever the Moon is up and the Stars come out."

And having got what information she could out of the giggler in the tree, Spite walked on, and presently met little Brisk, coming through the glade on her way to the Enchanted Bower, where she was going to gather rays off the wild white roses while the dew was on them. She stopped

when Spite spoke to her in a treacly voice and asked, " Who are you, my little dear ? "

" I am Brisk, Old Woman's little Maid," said she, and was passing on, when Spite caught her arm and detained her.

" Wait, my little dear—what hurry ? " said she. " I want to ask you if you have seen the fair Princess Trill taking her morning walks in Elfin Wood lately ? "

" She walks out with Prince Glee, Worry, and Dopple every morning," replied Brisk.

" And *never alone*, my little dear ? "

" *Never alone.*"

And so, as that was all she could learn from Brisk, Spite trudged on again, and in a very few minutes she reached Old Woman's House, made in the Hollow of the Ash-Tree ; and there was Old Woman spinning in the doorway, as hard as if she were spinning for her life. Spite accosted her in her treacly voice, and begged leave, as a weary wayfarer, to sit and rest.

" *Oil and vinegar*," said Old Woman,

who had a trick of saying what she thought aloud, as well as what she meant people to hear. " Yes, you may sit down on the pint-stoup, and rest, if you are tired. You should do as I do : I never stir from home, and so I am never tired."

" But I have the good of my fellow-creatures at heart, and one can't help them by sitting still," said Spite insinuatingly.

" I don't believe a word of *that*," thought Old Woman, aloud, and then she asked : " Pray, madam, whom are you going to benefit now ? "

Old Woman has her Doubts.

" The lovely Princess Trill."

" She'll do better without you," thought Old Woman again. " I shall drop her a word of caution."

" Ho ! ho ! will you, my worthy friend ! " said Spite to herself ; " I'll be beforehand with you ! " So up she rose from the pint-stoup, thanked Old Woman blandly for her hospitality, and resumed her journey. As she went out of sight, Old Woman, looking after her, thought aloud once more : " Fat and smooth as her face is, she has got a wonderful cast of Aunt Spite in her eyes." And then she went on spinning.

During the night, the Stranger from the Country, as Spite now called herself, made considerable way, and just as morning broke she entered on a glade of Elfin Wood, near the Queen's Hunting Palace, to which her Majesty and the Court had lately returned from the Air-Palace in the wooded chine of the rocks. From the distance she could see Whip and the inferior huntsmen bringing out the pack for exercise, and having no fancy to fall into their jaws, she waited where she was until the noisy troop had disappeared in another direction.

The Arrival at Elfin Court.

But even then any approach to the Palace was prevented by the fact of Dopple and Worry being left behind to keep guard at the gates with Watch and Spy ; so the Stranger from the Country was fain to sit down amongst the underwood, and wait for an eligible opportunity to slip into the Palace unobserved. She had to wait a long while, and feeling extremely hungry, she made a miserable breakfast off a toadstool, which disagreed with her so violently that she was almost in a mind to fling off her Mask of Pious Hypocrisy, and rush into the Palace in her own undisguised person. But the desire of revenge prevailed over this spasm of passion, and she resigned herself to her suffering with as much resolution as would come to her aid.

She had got over her worst anguish when her attention was called off by seeing Dopple and Worry jump up and wag their tails, and run to and fro in great joy to welcome Prince Glee and Princess Trill, who were just issuing from the Palace Gates to take their morning walk. When these rapturous greetings were over, all four turned to come up the glade at the end of which the Stranger from the Country was crouching amongst the underwood. Dopple came first, turning her sharp nose hither and thither to snuff out an enemy ;

Spite sees the Royal Couple.

behind her followed Prince Glee and Princess Trill, arm in arm ; and Worry brought up the rear with much demonstration of fuss and consequence. Now, Worry and Dopple had received a special commission from Fairy Queen herself to keep an eye on Princess Trill, and never to lose sight of her until she was safely married to Prince Glee, and ready to set sail with him to the Isle of Palms, where he had been presented to the appointment of Master of the Revels ; and the two worthy animals performed their duty with true canine fidelity.

Fears for her Safety.

As they drew near to where she was concealed, the Stranger from the Country began to experience some anxiety for her personal safety if she did not promptly meet the danger face to face. So up she rose, shook out her cloak, rearranged her hood, and smiling her oiliest, advanced towards the lovers. When Dopple perceived this sudden apparition, she gave a low growl of warning, and Worry immediately sprang forward, and with his companion instituted a searching examination of the feet and ankles of the Stranger from the Country, much to her terror and discomfort, for every moment she expected to feel their teeth meeting through her skin and bone—she had no flesh worth mentioning. But the animals thought better of it, and when Princess Trill sang out in her sweetest voice, " To heel, Worry ; quiet, good Dopple ! " on the instant they were obedient and retired to their proper positions.

The Stranger from the Country, thankful for this deliverance, bowed to Princess Trill, who returned the courtesy with some hurry and reluctance.

" Dear Prince Glee ! " whispered she breathlessly, " do you see anything in that person's face which reminds you of Aunt Spite ? I thought she glanced at me with a very malignant eye, notwithstanding her smiles."

Princess Trill's Terror, and

" She is an odious-looking creature ;

Prince
Glee's
Reas=
surance.

but I do not see a likeness to Aunt Spite, my precious love ; so calm your fears, hush your tremulous palpitations," replied Prince Glee tenderly. " Aunt Spite, you know, is safe at Castle Craft."

For all this reminder and encouragement, Princess Trill could not help looking back over her shoulder two or three times to see in what direction the Stranger from the Country went ; and her dismay was increased when she saw Spy and Watch bowing to her in a very conciliatory manner, and then unlocking the Palace gates for her admittance.

Yes, Spy and Watch, sharp as they were, were not sharp enough to see through the mask of Pious Hypocrisy which Spite wore under her hood ; and as it was a rule at Fairy Queen's Court to allot suites of apartments to distinguished Strangers from the Country who came up to witness grand festivals, she was immediately conducted to the elegant bower over the gate, from which she could watch the incomings and outgoings of every member of the Court.

She then sent round her card, and before the day was out half the dignitaries of the Royal Household, the principal members of the Society of Wiseacres, and all the *élite* of the wit and respectability of Elfin Court had paid her a visit of ceremony and gone away highly prepossessed in her favour. And that night the Stranger from the Country slept on thistle-down without a single thorn in her pillow.

Spite's gracious Reception.

SPITE'S INTERVIEW with FANCY, THE COURT MORALIST & STORY-TELLER

THE next morning, the Stranger from the Country was up betimes; and the first sound she heard was the Grand Pomp and his trumpeters blowing the alarm for all the Court to prepare to go out to the Picnic in Elfin Wood, where there was to be music and dancing on the greensward. It was with a spasm of acute disappointment that Spite now remembered the warning False-Pretences had given her; for she would dearly have liked to make herself smart, and to have gone abroad with the rest of

the pleasure-seekers; but as that could not
be without seriously imperilling the success
of the plot she had in hand, she resigned
herself to her fate, dressed herself in her
sad-coloured garments with the utmost care,
threw open the window of her bower, and
ensconced herself behind the curtain, to
watch the departure of the Royal train.

At that moment the provisions for
luncheon were just beginning to be packed
by the Court Cooks, and Spite saw hamper
after hamper of sweets brought forth at
the gates and put into the carriages.
Already, too, the gay young sparks were
gathering in knots, and waiting for the
coming of the Queen and her pretty Maids
of Honour. Spite recognised many of
these juvenile Fairies, and bowed to them
with much condescension. There was
Frolic waiting for Clipsome, and Wink
waiting for Dot, and Dump waiting for
Touchy; there was old Tippet, in a new
cloak of coquelicot, waiting for some
sparkling Elf to fall in love with him;

Prepa=
rations
for the
Picnic.

10

there was Tippity Wichet and his Brothers ;
there was Trip, Try-for-it, Finick, Turn,
Twist, Lush, and Trap on the lookout for
Blue-bell, Satin, Sleek, Sly, Flip, Arch,
Mite, and Dimple ; there was Tricksy with
Quip and Crank, and a great many more
besides, too numerous to mention.

Spite watched the gay and happy crowd
with very envious feelings, until the great
gates below the window of her bower were
flung wide open, and, with soft music
preceding her, Fairy Queen came forth.

The
Start for
Elfin
Wood,
and

Her Majesty rode a white butterfly,
and was immediately followed by Mother
Dignity on a humble bee ; Prince Goldheart rode at his Royal Mistress's right
hand upon a spirited dragon-fly ; and
Muffin, Master of the Ceremonies, rode at
her left, mounted on a beetle.

Next came Princess Trill and Prince
Glee, in apparel of gossamer and silver,
mounted on golden-winged moths ; and
then followed, two and two, the Maids of
Honour and the Royal Pages riding upon

young flies. The Knights-Fairy of the
Guard rode armed cockchafers ; and the
gay young Fairies whom Spite had seen
collecting before the Royal train appeared,
now mounted their respective steeds, and
galloped off in the dust kicked up by the
cockchafers. There were still a few left
behind, however. There was Hedgehog,
the family coach of the three sisters, Snip,
Snap, and Snarl ; and when those elderly
Elves were driving slowly off, they saw
Tippet, and invited him to take a seat
behind ; which, with a singularly bad
grace, he did. Then there was Dump,
who got very slowly under weigh in his
country-built carriage of a snail-shell,
drawn by a grey, obstinate snail ; and
there was Tippity Wichet and his Brothers,
who found their drag, with its team of
eight wrong-headed wasps, almost more
than they could manage ; and besides
these, there were numerous members of
the Royal Society of Wiseacres, who,
being but little accustomed to equestrian

The
Vagaries
of the
various
Steeds.

exercises, were carried off by their respective spiders into remote nooks of Elfin Wood, where it is to be feared they saw very little indeed of the Picnic.

But at last they were all off, and the Courtyard of the Hunting Palace echoed only to the monotonous tread of the sentinels, Watch and Spy. In this state of things the Stranger from the Country began to feel very melancholy, and to long for some private diversion ; so she left her bower, and after straying some time through the deserted apartments of the Palace, she came by chance upon the Royal Theatre, where the Mimes, under the direction of Fancy, the Court Moralist and Story - Teller, were preparing the Pantomime for the evening's entertainment.

Fancy bowed, and begged her to remain, as she was about to retire with an air of being exceedingly shocked and horrified.

" There is no harm here, madam, I assure you ! " cried he good-humouredly ; " you permit a heated and ignorant imagina-

tion to run away with you. Pray attend
our Pantomime, and you will learn henceforward not to condemn or deride us."

" I will consider of it," said the Stranger
from the Country ; " but all my principles
are against frivolous amusements."

" Madam, it seems to me that I know
your voice," said Fancy reflectively ; " I
also discern something familiar in your
visage."

" Sir, you are mistaken. You and I
never met before ; our connections and
pursuits are totally distinct," replied the
Stranger sharply.

" Certainly, madam, certainly. But do
you happen to know the Fairy of the
Enclosed Garden on the borders of Sheneland, where the Sun never shines ? " asked
Fancy.

" No, sir ; I do not own the acquaintance of any such person."

" Permit me to return with you to
your bower, and tell you her story," said
Fancy ; " you have a long day before

Fancy ques= tions Spite.

you, and as I have now seen all put in train for the Pantomime of this evening, I should be very glad to give some time to your service."

" I do not want to hear any of your nonsense," snapt the Stranger from the Country, forgetting her assumed character.

" Madam, you must then hear how Truth plucked the Mask from the Face of Pious Hypocrisy," urged Fancy significantly.

" No, sir, I would rather hear the first story you named," replied the Stranger, now humbly enough ; and she quaked all over with the dread of discovery. So Fancy, the Royal Moralist, accompanied her to her bower, and told her the tale of the " Enclosed Garden, where the Sun never Shines."

Fancy
tells
another
Tale.

The Enclosed Garden, where the Sun never Shines.

" On the borders of Sheneland there is an Enclosed Garden, where the sun never shines, and in which lives a woman alone —always alone, with the great walls built up to the sky, and never a summer day to warm her all the year round. She walks to and fro in the cold shadow, generally with her chin on her breast, and her eyes downcast, muttering to herself, ' *It is all my own—it is all my own ;* ' but, now and then, she looks forward and outward, and then her face shows narrow, and thin, and bitter, and when she says, ' It is all my own,' again, an ugly laugh twists her lips, as if she were laughing at herself.

" In the Enclosed Garden there are many things beautiful to the eye, but they want the genial sun to make them as beautiful as they might be.

" There are clustered roses, but they are quite pale—not one crimson blush amongst them all ; there are fine fruits hanging on the trees, but they are crude and sour, and would set your teeth on edge if you tried to eat them. In the midst of this abundance, the woman, who goes to and fro, muttering, ' It is all my own —it is all my own,' is starving inch by inch. Now and then she ceases the doleful triumph, and makes a snatch at the robe covering her sapless breast ; under it her heart lies cold as any stone ; and then she says, ' What is it all worth ! ' and a mocking Fairy voice answers back from beyond the wall, ' Nothing—*but it is all thy own.*' Then with her nails she tries

How Avarice is pun= isbed.

to pick the mortar out between the stones, and to peer through a chink at what lies outside her garden, but she only wounds her hands and fails ; so then she betakes herself again to the solemn pacing to and fro, with hunger gnawing at her throat, with her heart lying in her breast cold as any stone, and muttering as she goes in the same monotonous, miserable voice, ' It is all my own—it is all my own ; but what is it worth ! ' and the Fairy mocks her beyond the wall with, ' Nothing— *but it is all thy own.*'

It is all
my own—
It is all
my own.

" Once upon a time, where the Enclosed Garden lies now, stood a little cottage, in which lived a woodman and his wife and their three daughters. The name of the eldest was Clutch, the name of the second was Waste, and the name of the third was Frail.

" This woodman and his wife were very decent, honest, hard-working people ; he went out to his labours in the forest every morning at daybreak and did not return till the sun went down ; but his wife stayed at home, guided the house and took care of the children.

The honest Woodman and his Wife.

" Now each of these three children had a Fairy godmother who had given her her own name. Fairy Clutch was Clutch's godmother, Fairy Waste was Waste's godmother, and Fairy Frail was Frail's godmother. Their father and mother loved Frail the best because she was little and weak and often in trouble ; and they loved Clutch the least because she was rough and strong, and was always thinking how much good she could do for herself, and how little she could do for anybody else. As for Waste, she wandered about the woods like a wild thing, and was sometimes missing for days and days together ; but when she had eaten all she carried away and was hungry, then she came back to the cottage, led by the lamp that always burnt in the window after nightfall, and, tapping on the glass, she begged to be taken in. Her father always rose and opened the door, and her mother kissed her, and said, 'Some night, Waste, there will be no light in the pane when thou art seeking thy way home, and thou wilt go astray into the thick forest, where wild beasts will fall upon thee and devour thee.'

Waste the Wan=derer, Little Frail, and

"But Waste only laughed and warmed herself at the fire, while her mother dried her clothes, and Frail, who had a loving heart, brought out bread, and milk, and honey, to refresh her sister. All this time Clutch would sit straight up by the hearth, with her narrow garments tucked about her heels, her lips pinched, her brows bent, and her eyes full of gloom, thinking, in her bad heart, ' This is the way my father and mother waste their substance ; there will be little enough for any of us when they die ; ' and every morsel of food that went down poor Waste's throat she begrudged as if it were a piece of gold out of her own portion ; but Waste only ate the more, to vex her.

"All round the cottage there was a pretty, plain place, where the trees of the forest had been cut down, and fine fruit-trees planted in their stead, with scented flowers and shrubs, and useful medicinal herbs in patches between them. Frail liked to lie on the grass in the sunshine, half hearing the sounds of the bees and the birds in the branches, while she drowsed through the long summer day ; Waste liked to shake the blossoms down when they were full, and to cover Frail with the white and rosy leaves ; but Clutch let her fruit hang till it was ripe, then she gathered

Their Greedy Sister, Clutch.

how Waste and Frail loved the Sum= mer, and

it, and stored it in sacks, in a safe place, and locked it up, and let nobody get at it; and there it lay till it rotted. Whatever Clutch laid her hands upon was never of use to anyone, for she could not endure to see her gatherings lessen, and if any person was so ill advised as to come near to take some by force, she let loose upon them in an instant her ugly mastiff, Greed, and cried out in a rage, ' It is all my own—it is all my own ! '

Clutch loved only Gain.

" Now it came to pass that at length the woodman and his wife died. The mother died the first, and then the father. Before the father died he called his three daughters round his bed, and spoke to them as follows :—

" ' Clutch, thou art the eldest, and to thee I leave it in charge to do justice to thy sisters, Waste and Frail. Be thou patient and forgiving with Waste, and be thou watchful and loving with Frail.'

The Dying Wood- man's Trust, and

" Then Clutch wept Crocodile's tears, and cried, ' O father ! I will—I will.'

" Then the woodman, believing her, said, ' Here is the cottage and garden : let them be divided into three portions, and agree amongst yourselves for the first choice : only take care of Frail, for she was her mother's own child ; and don't let Waste starve, because I loved her.' And so the old man died.

" As soon as he was buried, Clutch divided the garden into *two* equal parts, and calling Waste and Frail to witness, said, ' See what I have done : *that*,' pointing to the left, ' is for you two, and *this*,' pointing to the right, ' is for me, too.'

How Clutch fulfilled it.

" Waste measured the land shrewdly with her eye, and said, ' Nay, but, Sister Clutch, this is not fair. Our father told thee to make *three* portions of his inheritance, and thou hast made but *two*, and taken the better for thine own.'

" ' I knew there would be strife,' cried Clutch, in a rage ; ' it is ill dealing with knaves and fools—let us part. Tell me what thou wilt take for thy share.'

" Then Waste, who had little mind to live under her elder sister's niggard rule, bartered her portion of the land for so much bread, honey, and wine, and having filled her wallet, she kissed Frail, and went out at the cottage door to seek her a new home.

" No sooner was Waste gone, than Clutch cried out to Frail, ' Come, Lazybones, up and work : there shall be no folded hands where I rule.'

" So poor Frail, though she was little and weak, got up and did her best ; but the sun was very hot in the midday, and presently Frail came creeping to her sister's side, and prayed, ' Dear Clutch, let me rest ! ' But Clutch was angry, and shook her roughly by the arm, saying, ' Thou art idle ; thou art idle. Waste is gone— come, tell me what thou wilt take for thy share of the land, and thou shalt begone too.'

" ' Only give me Peace,' said Frail ; ' and freedom from thy bitter bondage ! '

and on that, Clutch thrust her also to the door, and she went away feebly into the cool shade of the forest.

"Then Clutch clapped her hands, and cried, '*It is all my own! It is all my own!*' and in came her Fairy godmother, and they had a long talk about it; the ugly mastiff, Greed, sitting between them and listening with cocked ears to every word they said.

"'I'll build a wall round it, so that nobody shall be able to see over,' cried Clutch, in high glee; 'then the fruit will never be stolen, and I shall have plenty to store up, if I live a hundred years. There was no telling where things went, as long as Waste and Frail were in the house; but now I shall have everything in my own way, because it is all my own!'

"Then her Fairy godmother patted Clutch's ugly head, and declared that she was a child after her own heart.

"The next day Clutch began to build, and her godmother helped her with right goodwill, while Greed kept watch to worry

The
Building
of the
Wall,

Waste and Frail if they should venture to come by that way again. Before winter arrived the wall was pretty nearly breast high, but when the snow was on the ground they ceased building, and Greed slept by a starved fire indoors; while Clutch reckoned up every evening how rich she would be, if she lived a hundred years, and had every year a good fruit harvest. The result of this calculation always put Clutch into such high good-humour that she would give Greed, who commonly had to fare for himself, and was consequently lean and savage enough, *all* her potato-skins, and *all* her cheese-parings; *all* was not *quite* a feast, but Greed was so famished that he would thankfully have eaten his own tail had it not been too short to admit of a bite.

" Now it happened one night the snow fell so thickly, that Clutch, looking out of the window, could see nothing but a white curtain driven across and across it, before the wind, but she could hear something which sounded like a cry beyond the wall.

And bow it pro=
gressed.

Listening, she knew it was her sister Frail. Frail was weeping faintly, and now and then she raised her voice, and cried out, ' Clutch ! Clutch ! I was my mother's own child ! Take me out of the storm ! O Clutch ! it is so cold, and I have had nothing to eat since the snow began to fall yesterday.' At which Clutch laughed, and looked so ugly, that even Greed snarled at her. There was silence for a minute or two, and then the wail recommenced : ' O Clutch, dear Clutch ! give me a corner by thy fire, and a crust of bread ! ' But Clutch only laughed again, shut to the window, and said, ' Not I ! *It is all my own !* '

"And the next morning, when the Fairy godmother came in, she said to the child after her own heart, ' Clutch, there's a pretty log lying by the wall that the snow has covered ; go, thou, and dig it out. It will make us a rare fire.'

"So Clutch took her shovel and called Greed to help, bidding him scratch the snow away ; but Greed would only sit on his stump of a tail and howl till the whole forest echoed again. And when Clutch had shovelled the log clear, behold it was her sister Frail,—her mother's own child,— and she was dead. Then Clutch wept Crocodile's tears over her, and said she was very sorry ; but at night she comforted herself with calculations.

" When the winter was gone, Clutch and her Fairy godmother set to work on the wall again, and the fame of what they were doing went abroad throughout all Sheneland, and brought many people from far and near to behold the works.

Good
Advice
scorned.
" ' Take care, Clutch, or thou wilt build out the sun, and then, who will ripen thy fruit for thee ? ' cried an old man, who had seen the wisdom and folly of many things.

" ' I do but build out thieves and robbers, and may I not do what I will with mine own ? ' replied Clutch, heaving up a great stone.

" ' If thou wouldst build out thieves, thou must build out thyself,' cried another.

'Who robbed Waste and Frail of their inheritance ? Who left little Frail to die in the snow ? '

"But Clutch only scoffed at them, and built on. And by and by, when she was one day hard at work, she heard a voice which she knew ; and it was Waste calling to her.

" ' Clutch ! Clutch ! art thou there ? ' she cried.

" So Clutch, who was high on a ladder, looked over and saw Waste all in rags, and very thin, miserable, and travel-worn. Clutch laughed at the piteous sight, and asked her sister what she wanted.

The
Return
of
Waste,
and

" ' Take me home and let me rest, dear Clutch,' said Waste ; ' I have been in far lands and can teach thee new ways of growing rich.'

"But Clutch replied, ' I like my own way best.'

" ' Then I will work for thee for a wage,' said Waste, looking up with thin, starved face.

" ' Nay ; for thou wouldst destroy more than thou couldst earn.'

" ' I will be thy slave for a little bread to eat and a little water to drink,' pleaded Waste.

" But Clutch only grinned her ugly grin that made Greed snarl, and said nothing.

" ' Then give me a morsel of food, because my father loved me,' urged Waste, with tears in her hollow eyes ; but Clutch shook her head, and only went down the ladder for more mortar.

" ' Where is my sister, little Frail ? ' cried Waste again.

" ' Go to the lily-bed by the water-course, and there thou wilt find her.'

" So Waste dragged herself feebly to the lily-bed by the water-course, but no Frail was there—only something in shape like a grave, and ragged grass waving on it.

" And the next day, when the Fairy godmother went to see Clutch again, she said, ' Coming by Frail's grave, I found these bits of clothing, and there were certain bones strewn there as of one torn by wolves.'

" ' It has been as our mother said! The wild beasts of the forest have fallen on Waste, and devoured her!' and Clutch wept Crocodile's tears again, but she laughed in her heart, for now she was sure that she should never be disturbed in possession of her inheritance.

"⸱But she soon discovered that she should not be nearly as happy as she expected, and her Fairy godmother found her such dull company that at last she went away and left her to herself. The next misfortune was, that one night Greed died in his sleep, and though Clutch still went on making her calculations, she had no comfort in them any longer.

Ill-gotten Gains turn to Dross.

" And a mocking Fairy set up her bower in the sunshine over the wall, and mocked her as she walked about counting her harvest, and saying, '*It is all my own— it is all my own*;' for Clutch is the miserable

woman in the Enclosed Garden on the Borders of Sheneland, where the Sun never shines."

"*Now*, Madam, do you know my Fairy?" asked Fancy, when he had finished his narrative.

"No, sir, I do not," replied the Stranger from the Country.

"But you will know her some day, Madam. She calls cousins with Spite and Pious Hypocrisy, and they generally end their days with her."

"That is no concern of mine—I do not intermeddle with the concerns of strangers," said Spite, gaining a little courage from the very imminence of her danger. She felt sure Fancy had his suspicions about her; or why should he have told her such a dismal legend?

"Do you not?" said the Court Moralist. "That is a good principle to go upon, but I believe I have heard it rumoured that you are hand and glove with Specious, Plausible, and False-Pretences."

" Nothing of the kind, sir ; I am a simple Stranger from the Country, and never was at the Mask-sellers' in my life," cried Spite, trembling.

" Indeed, Madam—then I will leave you until I can have the pleasure of seeing Truth tear the Mask from the Face of Pious Hypocrisy. When that instructive scene takes place you will be present, Madam. I wrote the Plot of the Piece a long while ago, but it will be more interesting to you to see the play played than to hear it merely recited. And so I will now take my leave, for I hear the trumpets which herald the return of Fairy Queen and the Royal Train from the Picnic."

Gives Spite an Invitation.

So Fancy, the Court Moralist and Story-Teller, withdrew, and left the Stranger from the Country shaking in her shoes and grinding her teeth in the extremity of her fear. That horrible sensation lasted until the Courtyard of the Hunting Palace was all astir, and her curiosity tempted her to look out again. Then in her rage at the sight of Princess Trill blushing like a red rose as Prince Glee assisted her to alight from her golden-winged moth, she forgot her own perils, and said to herself with bitter determination, " Come what will, there shall be no wedding to-morrow ! *there shall be no wedding to-morrow !* "

Spite's Wicked Pro= phecy.

And all that evening, while Fairy Queen and her Court were at the Pantomime and the State Supper afterwards, Spite sat in the bower by herself, maturing the wicked plans which were to prevent it and throw all Elfin Court into mourning. But that night when she went to bed there was a whole forest of thorns in her pillow of thistledown, and not one wink of sleep did she get for thinking of the time when she might no longer call Castle Craft her own, and when she might be placed under the parsimonious house-keeping of Mistress Clutch who lived in the Enclosed Garden on the Borders of Sheneland where the Sun never shines.

R.K.

HOW THE CONSPIRACY OF THE MASK-SELLERS WAS QUITE SUCCESSFUL, & HOW PRINCESS TRILL WAS CARRIED OFF

THE next morning all Elfin Court woke up to the merry music of every bell in Sheneland ringing in the wedding-day of lovely Princess Trill and gallant Prince Glee.

In Princess Trill's beautiful bower were assembled all the four-and-twenty Maids of Honour, with Mother Dignity at the head of them, to help to array her in her bridal robes ; and at the same time Prince Glee was being dressed in his bridal garments by the four-and-twenty Royal Pages, with Muffin, Master of the Ceremonies, at the head of them.

The Hunting Palace had never been in such a bustle and fuss since it was a Palace, but Fairy Queen, for the love she bore sweet Princess Trill and her Cousin Prince Glee, put up with the disturbance with serene amiability, and while conversing with Prince Goldheart on affairs of state, she snatched a moment to send a message to the Princess's bower to the effect that she desired to see her and present her in person with a wedding gift as soon as her toilette was completed.

The Tiring of the Fair Princess.

When the messenger arrived, the Princess was just sitting down on a stool, for Mother Dignity, who was short and fat, to fasten the veil of dew-besprent gossamer upon her golden hair, crowned with white rose-buds from the Enchanted Bower. Mother Dignity suggested that it would be more respectful for the fair bride to receive her sovereign unveiled; so Princess Trill sent word back to the Queen that she was

ready, and in a very few minutes her
Majesty appeared.

The Queen carried in her hand a casket
of jewels, and taking Princess Trill aside,
she spread them before her, saying,
" Sweet Cousin, these are the best gifts
I can give thee as a bride. Here is the fair
Pearl of Meekness, the Emerald of Duty, the
Ruby of Love, and the Diamond of Purity.
Wear them, and be happy." And with
that the Queen kissed her and withdrew.

Then the four-and-twenty Maids of
Honour gathered about Princess Trill again
and extolled her gifts, and Mother Dignity
put the Pearl of Meekness over her fore-
head, and the Emerald of Duty in her hand,
and the Ruby of Love on her lips, and the
Diamond of Purity on her heart, and then
bade her sit down on the stool again, and
let her fasten the veil of dew-besprent
gossamer over her golden hair ; for a
message had come from Prince Glee to
say that he was dressed, and all the wedding
was ready, and only waiting for her.

Just at this moment, however, there came another interruption in the shape of Flat, a Court Usher. Mother Dignity was quite put out by the delay, and asked sharply what he wanted. To this Flat replied, that a benevolent Stranger who had come up from the Country only yesterday, besought it as a favour on which more than her life depended that she might have five minutes' conversation with Princess Trill alone before she was married. It would have been a very uncourteous thing for a bride to refuse so simple a grace as this ; so the Princess in her dulcet voice ordered the Stranger from the Country to be shown into her inner bower, and putting aside the veil which Mother Dignity still held in her hands, she went to speak to her visitor.

When Princess Trill appeared before the benevolent Stranger from the Country, she was all over one blush of loveliness, and that person started back quite amazed, and was not mistress of her parts of speech

Princess Trill's Courtesy.

for several seconds, so great was her
astonishment and vexation at the sight;
but when Princess Trill looked up in the
benevolent Stranger's face, and saw that
she was the person whom she and Prince
Glee had met in Elfin Wood, she was
ready to sink to the ground with terror;
for instead of wearing only a broad,
treacly smile, the Stranger now allowed
a malicious gleam of triumph to shine out
of her green eyes.

"Fair Princess, I have brought you a
gift from a venerable relative of yours who
is prevented by urgent private affairs from
assisting at your marriage," said the
Stranger from the Country; and before
Princess Trill could recover herself sufficiently to resist, or raise her voice to call
for help, she had drawn the Mask of Spite's
face from under her cloak and fastened
it tight on under the hapless bride's
golden hair.

The transformation wrought in that
instant was so complete and withal so

Spite
carries
out her
plan

ludicrous that Pious Hypocrisy laughed very much like Spite in a mood of high gratification, and then asked the Princess, who was quite unaware of her own appearance and only felt a little stiffness about the mouth, if she could carry back any thanks or compliments to her venerable relative.

Entirely success= fully.

Princess Trill said " No," being only anxious to get rid of her disagreeable visitor and to return to her friends as quickly as possible.

" Then I will bid you farewell ; and if you remember any message after I am gone you can come down into Elfin Wood and seek me near the hollow trunk of the Ash-Tree, in which Old Woman lives with her little Maid Brisk." And with that the Stranger from the Country pretended to retire, but in reality she only hid herself behind the window-curtain to witness what sort of a reception Princess Trill would receive when she presented herself before her companions with Aunt Spite's face.

She met a very strange and rude reception indeed : Mother Dignity stared with stupid amazement at her audacity, and the young Maids of Honour began to titter and whisper to each other, saying, " The ridiculous, ugly old *thing*! And to come tricked out for all the world like a *bride*! Gossamer of silver, and white roses from the Enchanted Bower! Well, I'm sure, *they* will go out of fashion if Aunt Spite is to be allowed to come to Court in them. Oh! what a perfect fright! "

Princess Trill saw the skittish looks and heard the hard words all round her, but she said meekly, " Mother Dignity, give me my veil; we are keeping Prince Glee waiting."

Princess Trill's humiliation, and

At this all the assemblage burst into a peal of laughter, and Mother Dignity bounced out of the bower, shrieking, " Aunt Spite has come to Court and impudently claims to be sweet Princess Trill! " and then fell into violent hysterics.

In a moment came running Prince Glee,

the Queen, Prince Goldheart, Muffin, the Royal Pages, and a vast body of people besides ; but as one after another they caught sight of the grinning Mask of Aunt Spite in the doorway, they stopped short and hung back. Prince Glee betrayed the utmost anger and disgust both in his countenance and his expressions. He turned away from the unhappy Princess with a scowl of aversion, while her Majesty spoke on the instant and with the utmost severity.

Prince Glee's Cruel Treatment of her.

" Spite, you are forbidden to appear at Elfin Court on any pretence : if you are not out of sight in five minutes you will be removed by the Guards to the Lock-up," said she.

Then was the Princess reduced to despair ; she turned and fled, everybody falling back from her steps as if her robes were tainted ; and as she came to the gates Wink put a bucket in her way, over which she stumbled and fell prostrate. Instead of helping her, the sentinels only laughed, and nobody showed any sympathy for her fate except Dopple and Worry, who seemed puzzled, for they came and licked her hands and feet, but when they saw her face they ran back howling disconsolately. And when the Princess regained her feet, almost blind with tears and utterly heartbroken, she went her way down the glade of Elfin Wood, and at the moment her foot crossed the threshold of the Palace all the Fairy joybells in Sheneland suddenly ceased ringing, and Old Woman, who was spinning as usual at her doorway in the Hollow of the Ash-Tree, lifted up her head and listened, saying anxiously, " There'll be no wedding to-day ; the Fairy-bells are silent ! "

The Bells cease Ringing.

No sooner had the supposed Aunt Spite been thus ignominiously driven away, than Prince Glee cried out in great haste and heat, " Where *is* Princess Trill ? " and immediately Mother Dignity recovered and bounced into the bower, and called— " Princess Trill ! Princess Trill ! the bene-

12

volent Stranger from the Country must spare you now, for Prince Glee is waiting for you ! ''

But no Princess Trill was there to answer ; and Mother Dignity fainted flat on the spot. Then came in Prince Glee, and the Queen herself, and Prince Gold-heart, and all the Maids of Honour, and all the Royal Pages, and the excitement grew and became tremendous.

They searched the bower through and through ; they went over the Palace from one end to the other ; Prince Glee crying all the time on the name of his dear Princess, and imploring her to answer him. But it was all in vain. There was no wedding that day, for there was no bride, and all Elfin Court was thrown into mourning.

Mourn= ing in the Palace.

Still the quest went on unceasingly ; but night fell and the Princess was not found. Then said Prince Glee, '' It is her Aunt Spite again who has beguiled her away ; by this time, no doubt, she has her locked up in the dismallest dungeon of

CARRIED·HER·AWAY·
THROUGH·THE·WILDEST·
WILDS·OF·ELFIN·WOOD

Castle Craft ! " And his heart sank within him, for the grief and disappointment of his loss were very hard to bear.

Fairy Queen was troubled beyond expression at this dolorous ending to her scheme of happiness, but after a little talk with Prince Goldheart, she touched the bereaved Prince Glee on the shoulder, and said, " Take heart, my Cousin, to-morrow you shall have a band of Guards, and you shall set out to effect the deliverance of the sweet and hapless Princess. Tuflongbo returns to-night from his mission to the Puffraspabi and the Alicompagni, and he will accompany you."

So Prince Glee went to bed, and while he was sleeping, the benevolent Stranger from the Country bound Princess Trill hand and foot and carried her away through the wildest wilds of Elfin Wood, far beyond Castle Craft, and left no trace behind her.

The Queen consoles Prince Glee.

PRINCE GLEE & TUFLONGBO
SET OUT IN PURSUIT OF
PRINCESS TRILL

THE next morning Prince Glee arose
with a heavy sense of misfortune
on his mind, and as soon as he was
dressed he went away to the stables, to see
that his darling steed, Swift-and-Sure, which
had helped him in his flight from Castle Craft
with the rescued Princess once before, was
in condition for a long and arduous journey.
On the way he fell in with the great
Traveller Tuflongbo, wearing his cloak of
peacocks' eyes, and they immediately got
into conversation. Tuflongbo condoled
with Prince Glee on his bereavement, and

180

said, if it would be any consolation to him, he would show him a new beetle, which he had discovered in the country of the Puffraspabi ; but poor Glee declined the entomological specimen, and replied that he had no heart for anything but setting out in pursuit of the lost Princess ; and that now he was on his road to see that his beloved Swift-and-Sure was fit for the journey.

"My dear fellow, this is a secret service ; let me earnestly advise that you go on foot," exclaimed Tuflongbo. "Whether a journey be taken for pleasure or for business, you cannot have too few encumbrances. If I could travel with nothing but a walking-stick, I should enjoy myself twice as much ! "

"But when I find the Princess, how am I to escape with her ? " asked Prince Glee.

"Trust to the chapter of accidents, as I do ! " replied Tuflongbo. "My excellent fellow, do you suppose I should have discovered the use to which the Old Moons

Tuflongbo's Good Counsel, and

are put if I had thought about how I was to descend from the high wall of stone and brick at World's End, after I had got to the top of it ? Should I have found the Aplepivi, and introduced their delicious fruit and golden honey into Sheneland, if I had waited for a boat to carry me across the sea that was three sights over ? Should I now have brought home a signed treaty of commerce with the Puffraspabi and the Alicompagni, if I had not ventured through the hedges of cactus, prickly pear, and fretful porcupine with which they fortify their country ? No, thrice NO, my Prince ! " And in the vehemence of his eloquence and demonstrations Tuflongbo rose on tiptoe and expanded visibly.

Prince Glee caught his enthusiasm, and turning back to the Palace, he said he would just pick his band of Guards, and be off immediately.

His Contempt for Prince Glee's Plans.

At this Tuflongbo's face expressed some disgust and contempt. "*Guards !* " said he, curling his lips, " what do you want with *Guards*? My dear Glee, you may be a Prince, but, excuse my plain speaking, you are certainly a *goose*. If you want to be betrayed, take a long tail with you ; if you want to give Aunt Spite warning when you are at hand, take a trumpet, perhaps *two* would be better, and a kettle-drum or so! Guards! Why, didn't the Knights-Fairy turn and leave you the last time when they met the Grand Pomp and Queen's Heralds proclaiming a Ball at Elfin Court ? "

put not your faitb in Guards.

"Truly they did," replied Prince Glee despondingly.

"Then what dependence can be placed on them again ? Feather-heads that forsake the path of honour and enterprise, to dance to a fiddle with one string! Now, seriously, Prince Glee, if you mean to find Princess Trill this time, you must have done with all nonsense. You must leave your royalty behind you ; you must dispense with Guards and beloved steeds ; and you must take ME with you, as Fairy Queen suggested to you last night, and to me also, in an interview that I had with her for the purpose of presenting the gifts and homage of the Puffraspabi and Alicompagni."

Prince
Glee's
Grati=
tude and
Jm=
patience.

"Dear Tuflongbo, your advice and your companionship are the best in the world," cried Prince Glee gratefully. "Come, let us start at once!" and the impetuous Prince tried to twist the great Traveller round towards the glades of Elfin Wood; but Tuflongbo was not prepared for this. His experience in many lands had taught him to be a philosopher, who never hurried or worried himself, or started on any enterprise without looking well to his shoes, his staff, and his inner fortification.

"My excellent fellow, I *can't* go without breakfast," said he deprecatingly. "I'm not in love, if you are; and, besides, I have only my slippers on."

Prince Glee sighed, yielded reluctantly to Tuflongbo's representations, and permitted himself to be led back to his apartments to breakfast. Tuflongbo gave

I can't go with=
out my Break=
fast.

bachelor breakfasts every morning when he was at home ; and very free, easy, pleasant entertainments they were. His friends dropped in to hear and tell the daily news in the most unceremonious manner ; even the Queen herself would come, with Prince Goldheart, and the grave Professors, and, in short, everybody that was delightful. As it had got abroad that the popular traveller was to accompany Prince Glee in his pursuit of Princess Trill, his apartments were crowded with his acquaintance to take leave of him, and while he was still in the middle of his first cup of tea, Fairy Queen came in with Prince Goldheart and Mother Dignity, who looked very flabby after her two severe attacks of illness the day before.

"We are sorry to lose your society at Court so soon, Tuflongbo," said her Majesty graciously ; "but the value of your company to our cousin, Prince Glee, will be so great, that we are ready to resign you for his sake. We wish you every success ; and for the

Tuf=longbo's Bachelor Parties.

furtherance of the object you have in view, our faithful servant, Elf Transformation, has this moment sent a Magic Button, which Mother Dignity will now sew upon Prince Glee's coat. When the Button is Buttoned, the Prince will become invisible ; when his coat flies open, then he will appear as he does now."

Then Prince Glee sat down on a low stool, and Mother Dignity sewed the Magic Button on his coat, and, by the Queen's orders, buttoned it ; upon which the stool where the Prince had been sitting but a moment before became vacant, and Wink kicked it away into a corner. All the company laughed, but Tuflongbo cried out, " Come, Glee, unbutton your coat, and let us look at you again ! " and immediately Prince Glee reappeared, looking exceeding small.

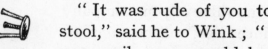

" It was rude of you to kick away the stool," said he to Wink ; " if I had not been very agile, you would have sent me into the corner too." So Wink apologised for having thoughtlessly insulted a friend in misfortune, and then harmony was restored, and the Prince took a cup of tea.

When breakfast was over, Tuflongbo said they had better lose no more time ; so his knapsack was brought in and strapped on his shoulders, and Prince Glee's knapsack was brought in and strapped on his shoulders ; then the Court Cobbler came in, and examined their shoes ; and Prince Goldheart presented each of them with a new walking-stick, and they went out at the Palace Gate, with the Queen and all the Court shaking hands with them. Spy and Watch had been removed for neglect of duty as sentinels, in allowing Princess Trill to be carried off ; but Dopple and Worry still hung about the steps, and when Prince Glee appeared, they ran to him, and licked his hands, and looked up in his face with tears in their eyes, and said, as plain as dogs could speak, " When you see dear Princess Trill, give our love to her, and tell her we are very sorry."

**Prepa=
rations
for the
Journey.**

**Worry's
Mes=
sage.**

And so the Travellers departed ; Mother Dignity, at the last moment, recovering sufficiently from a sudden attack of spasms, to throw an old shoe after them for luck.

PRINCE GLEE & TUFLONGBO
FALL into the HANDS of GIANTS

WHEN Prince Glee and Tuflongbo set
out in pursuit of Princess Trill, they
first followed the windings of the glade
that led past the hollow trunk of the Ash-
Tree in which lived Old Woman and her
little Maid Brisk. They were both at
home ; Old Woman spinning in the doorway and little Maid Brisk sorting out the
pink, and blue, and purple, and yellow silk
of flowers for Fairy Court-dress. Tuflongbo
stopped and asked if they had seen anybody
going by that way lately.

"There has been nobody this morning,"
replied Old Woman, "but late last night

two people passed just as Brisk was setting out to gather rays."

"What were they like?" asked Prince Glee, with eager curiosity.

"One was short and lean, with a broad fat face, full of creases of smiles. She wore a sad-coloured cloak, and a hood over her head."

"Ah! that was the benevolent Stranger from the Country," said Prince Glee.

"The other was tall and slender, and had Aunt Spite's face, crowned with roses, and robes of silver gossamer."

"Yes; that was wicked Aunt Spite herself, dressed up to come to Court——"

"Yet she wept and cried bitterly, and her voice was the voice of Princess Trill," said little Maid Brisk. "I followed them to the Enchanted Bower and heard it all the way."

"And the robes she wore were the very same robes I spun and wove for Princess Trill's wedding robes. The pattern was new, and I recognised it in a moment," said Old Woman, turning her wheel.

"My mind misgives me about that benevolent Stranger from the Country," remarked Tuflongbo. "I do not believe in benevolent Strangers from the Country. I am of opinion that this person with a broad fat face, and creases of smiles, in a sad-coloured cloak, and with a hood over her head, was a benevolent *Sham* from the Country, Prince Glee! Benevolent Strangers from the Country are not often seen in company with Aunt Spites. And I have my doubts about this person with Princess Trill's voice, and Aunt Spite's face, and Princess Trill's bridal crown and robes, being Aunt Spite at all."

"Don't speak in riddles, Tuflongbo, I implore you. If you are a clever fellow, prove it, and tell me what you believe!" said Prince Glee.

"I believe this, Prince Glee, and I'm sure of it!" replied the Traveller, wagging his head significantly. "I believe the benevolent Stranger from the Country was Aunt Spite herself in the mask of Pious

Hypocrisy, and that the tall slim thing in roses and silver gossamer was your own lost Princess Trill, half stifled under a mask made on the model of her Aunt Spite's own villainous countenance ! "

Old
Woman's
Approval
of his
Judg=
ment.
" You are a shrewd fellow, Tuflongbo," cried Old Woman approvingly. " You have hit on the truth. I have not sat by the roadside all these thousands of years, taking note of this, that, and the other, without being able to see through any disguise those Mask-sellers, Specious, Plausible, and False-Pretences, may invent. The benevolent Stranger from the Country *was* Aunt Spite, and the slim thing in the roses and silver gossamer *was* Princess Trill, weeping and heartbroken at being dragged away from Court and her dear Prince Glee."

" I drove her forth ; I, blind bat, mole, porpoise ; I drove her forth ! " cried Prince Glee distractedly. " Tuflongbo, what will be the end of this ? "

" The end of it, my dear fellow, will be,

that after various adventures, and various difficulties, we shall discover Princess Trill, that she will forgive you, and that you will marry her, and live happily ever afterwards!" replied Tuflongbo encouragingly.

"I am desperate! I, cruel monster, who loved her; I turned from her with aversion! The Queen addressed her severely, and I stood by; the Maids of Honour laughed at her, and Mother Dignity did not box their ears; Wink put a bucket in her way, and I did not kick him into the middle of next week! Oh! Tuflongbo, can she forgive me that? Can she, I say, forgive me *that*?"

"She wore Aunt Spite's face, and you did not know her—*that* will be your excuse, Prince Glee; therefore be comforted," said Old Woman kindly.

But Prince Glee would not be comforted; and when they left Old Woman and little Maid Brisk at the house made in the hollow trunk of the Ash-Tree, he buttoned up his

Prince Glee's Unhappiness.

13

coat, though Tuflongbo remonstrated with him, and said he might as well be walking with a *ghost* for company as with *him*, if he would be so churlish as to make himself *invisible*. He indulged his sorrow for ever so long ; but as Tuflongbo walked fast, and the sun was now up, he soon became heated, and after struggling with his feelings, he at last unbuttoned his coat, and became visible again.

Tuf= longbo's cheering help.

" You are not a bit like yourself, Prince Glee ; laugh and be merry ! " urged Tuflongbo pleasantly.

So Prince Glee brightened up, and they beguiled the way with cheerful conversation, until they came to the spot where Idle lay bound amongst the nettles, with the Wicked Fairy of the Creeping Plant with many Tendrils keeping guard over her. Tuflongbo divided the nettles, and looking in at the miserable little captive, said, " Idle, you have your ear to the ground and can hear a long way off. Did the two people who came by last night, just as little

Maid Brisk was setting out to gather rays, take the road that turns down beyond the Enchanted Bower into Tangle Wood ? "

"No," replied poor Idle. "I heard them, but they did not go into Tangle Wood."

Idle enlightens the Travellers.

"Did they follow the clue through the maze to Castle Craft ? " asked Tuflongbo.

"No. Oh, no ! They did not go to Castle Craft. They went through Rockpass towards Wildwaste, and then I lost all sound of them amongst the storms and earthquakes that are perpetually raging there."

"Then her Aunt Spite has carried Princess Trill away into the Country of the Giants ! " exclaimed Tuflongbo, greatly dismayed, and he and Prince Glee sat down and looked at each other for ever so long without speaking another word.

And well they might ; for indeed it was no common adventure to go to the rescue of a Stolen Princess in the Country of the Giants. Tuflongbo himself, though so ready to make light of difficulties, was the first to admit this.

Over the
hills
and far
away.
Prince
Glee
to the
Rescue.

" I did not expect to have to penetrate through Rockpass and Wildwaste, Prince Glee," was his remark. " This is a very different style of thing from going on a scientific discovery, or a peaceful mission to such tribes as the Aplepivi, Puffraspabi, and Alicompagni."

" So I suspect we shall find it, Tuflongbo," replied Prince Glee seriously.

" I have gone through some dangers in my time, but I never encountered a Giant with only a walking-stick before," said Tuflongbo. And then he and Prince Glee took another long stare at each other, and spoke never a word for nearly an hour.

While they were thus loitering away their time, the Wicked Fairy of the Creeping Plant with many Tendrils had slyly let down some of his cords, and tied Prince Glee's ankles together ; and he was just about to play Tuflongbo the same trick, when that sharp and active Traveller sprang to his feet, and flung a stone up at the grinning, ape-like creature, which caught him on the nose. He then released Prince Glee, and said they had better be moving on ; for they should never rescue Princess Trill by sitting there mooning at each other ; and, accordingly, they were just setting off, when poor little Idle cried out plaintively from amongst her nettles, " Tuflongbo, have you got anything good to eat in your knapsack ? "

" Yes," said Tuflongbo ; " I have got fruit of Aplepivi and golden honey."

" Oh ! do give me a spoonful of golden honey, it is so long since I tasted anything nice," implored poor Idle.

So Tuflongbo knelt down and put a spoonful of golden honey into her mouth, and then he gave her half of a fruit of Aplepivi ; but she could not get her hands loose to take it, and as soon as the great Traveller and Prince Glee were out of sight, the Wicked Fairy of the Creeping Plant with many Tendrils came down out

Tuflongbo's Kindness to Idle,

of the Tree and ate it before her face, saying at every bite, "Oh, Idle, how *luche de plaw* it is!" *Luche de plaw* being his peculiar idiom, signifying "how extremely delicious!"

And Prince Glee and Tuflongbo went on their journey again until they came to the Enchanted Bower blooming all over with wild white roses.

Tuflongbo stopped to examine it, and asked Prince Glee if he had ever come out there on Midsummer Eve with Fairy Queen's procession, to celebrate the Solemn Festival of the Maids from the Country under the Sun. Prince Glee had witnessed the ceremonial, but Tuflongbo had not, so the Prince gave him an account of it, and just as he came to the lot-drawing, a golden olive was flung to him by an invisible hand, and a voice in the air said, "So long as thou hast that golden olive, Prince Glee, thou wilt know neither hunger nor thirst."

"What a good gift!" said Tuflongbo;

" our honey and fruit of Aplepivi will soon be exhausted when we come to Wildwaste."

And after that the travellers went on again, gradually leaving behind them the lovely sylvan glades of Elfin Wood, where the birds sang like music, and the Fairy-bells rang in the moist and shady places, and the little springs bubbled up with joy in the sunshine.

At first the trees became few and scattered, and the grass scorched and brown ; then there was not even a bush to shelter a fly, or a blade of green upon the thirsty, rocky ground. The sky overhead was darkened like a black hood, and a long miserable wind blew out of the east and almost cut the travellers in two. Prince Glee's first impulse was to button up his coat, but Tuflongbo implored him to forbear. He said he had *not* heart to go through Rock-pass and Wildwaste with an invisible body beside him ; so Prince Glee let his coat fly wide open, and endured the bitter blast

Tuf-
longbo
loses
heart,
and

with silent fortitude. He was growing stronger and more courageous the more difficult appeared his task of rescuing Princess Trill, and after he had stood against that cruel east wind for a little while, he felt that no danger could daunt him afterwards, and Tuflongbo expressed himself as feeling the same sense of exhilaration and valour.

And now the road began to ascend, and to climb up, up, and up the steep stone-encumbered side of a hill lost at the top in thick clouds ; and by and by it also began to wind and to grow so narrow, with great towering cliffs on either hand, that the travellers had to separate and proceed singly. Then did Prince Glee feel thankful for the advice the experienced Tuflongbo had given him to leave Swift-and-Sure and the Knights-Fairy at home, for they would have been of far more hindrance than service to him now.

Prince Glee went first, and as he went his brave heart expanded, and turning round to Tuflongbo, who was behind him, he said, " Now know I that I follow on the track of sweet Princess Trill, for my breast swells with hope and anticipation."

" That is the way to look at it," replied Tuflongbo, puffing sorely ; " it is well to be jolly under all circumstances ; and so, dear Prince, don't you think we had better sit down under this pleasant precipice, and have our dinner ? "

Prince Glee acquiesced in this sensible proposal, and after they had refreshed themselves with fruit of Aplepivi and honey, they again trudged on their journey. The farther they went now, the higher grew the precipices, until they could scarcely see daylight ; and Tuflongbo said that they would soon come to the worst part of the Rockpass, and that Prince Glee might thank his stars he was young and slender, and not of such a mature plumpness as himself. And, indeed, Prince Glee did thank his stars, for before long they had to slip through the pass sideways, and

Onward, ever Onward.

from the groans of Tuflongbo it was clear the business was no joke for him. But the plucky, magnanimous little fellow made light of it, and when Prince Glee sighed a little too, he cheered him up with that golden proverb from the wisdom of the Country under the Sun, "Faint heart never won Fair Lady!" and Prince Glee remembered the lovely Princess Trill, and pushed on with redoubled ardour.

They had been travelling for about two hours in this arduous manner when they were both obliged to stop and take breath, and Prince Glee asked Tuflongbo if it was possible that her Aunt Spite could have brought the sweet Princess by this terrible road.

Prince Glee seeks Advice.

"There is no other way," replied Tuflongbo ; "so it is a comfort to reflect that the Princess, being tall and slight, would slip along easily, but Aunt Spite would be worse off than I am."

Then Prince Glee moved along again, with Tuflongbo following close behind, and at length the Rockpass began to open out, and all at once they emerged upon Wildwaste. Wildwaste was a vast gray tract of land, without a sign of vegetation upon its surface ; gloomy hills beyond hills enclosed it ; the sky overhead was one arch of thunder-clouds, and the air was full of dismal voices of Storm and Tempest, most awful to hear. They could see no living object far or near, but as they advanced cautiously into the exposed country they saw the earth continually heaving and opening around them, and the great scattered rocks quaked thereat like mere feathers.

" How that sweet heart Princess Trill must have trembled amidst these horrors ! " said Prince Glee, under his breath ; and for very pity he could almost have wept to remember that, in addition to these external sufferings, she had had to bear besides the recollection of his cruel words and looks of aversion. " But I'll make it up to her, I'll make it up to her, Tuflongbo, when I

his
Terror
for
Princess
Trill.

once get her safe out of her Aunt Spite's clutches, and carry her away to the pretty bower in the Isle of Palms!" cried he fervently, and he stepped over the stony ground of Wildwaste as if he were but just starting quite fresh in the morning. Tuflongbo could hardly keep up with him, and at last he was obliged to call a second halt.

Tuf= longbo's Wari= ness.

"We shall not get much farther to-night, Prince Glee," said Tuflongbo, as they sat down to rest in the midst of the weary waste ; "it is not safe travelling here after dark. Do you hear how the north wind is getting up ?"

"I hear it. And, Tuflongbo, am I mistaken in thinking I see one of those great rounded hills slowly moving towards us ?"

Tuflongbo started to his feet, sprang on a stone and looked out. As he looked, his face paled, and dropping softly down beside the Prince, he whispered, "We must be off, Glee ; that moving hill is no other

than Giant Slouchback, and he certainly
is coming this way."

So up jumped Prince Glee, and they were
just going to put their best foot foremost
and scurry off, when a huge hand was
stretched out and caught each of them by
the nape of his neck. They had been
sitting in the lap of Giant Slink, and never
knew it until they were seized in the vice
of his finger and thumb, and crammed
down into a deep dungeon of a pocket.
Their hearts beat audibly, but in the
darkness of their prison each grasped the
other's hand, and vowed to be faithful
until death ; which event seemed not very
far distant.

When he had got the hapless travellers
safe, Giant Slink set off trotting at the rate
of three hundred and sixty-five miles an
hour, and was presently joined by his
brother Giants, Slouchback and Lumba.
Up-hill and down-dale it was a sorry
shaking poor Prince Glee and Tuflongbo
had in Slink's pocket, until he reached the

The
Coming
of Slink,
and

his
Capture
of the
Prince
and his
Com=
panion.

great cavern in which he lived ; when, to add to their miserable discomfort, he immediately sat down to supper with Slouchback and Lumba, and left them to take their chance of being smothered in their dungeon.

The talk of the Giants over their supper was like the rumbling of thunder, but when Prince Glee grew accustomed to their voices, he distinguished his own name and that of Tuflongbo, and presently made out that Aunt Spite had retained these three Giants in her service, and that they had got Princess Trill shut up somewhere very safe indeed. He learnt also that Aunt Spite having thus made her poor niece secure, did not propose to remain in Wildwaste, but was going home to Sheneland by the earliest opportunity. It appeared, however, that it was necessary to consult her as to what should be done with the new prisoners Giant Slink had caught, so Slouchback went out and called her, and presently the wicked old thing

The Conver=sation at Wild=waste.

WE·HAVE·BROUGHT
YOU·THE·TWO·LITTLE
BIRDS, AUNT·SPITE

appeared wearing her Mask of Pious Hypocrisy.

Neither Prince Glee nor Tuflongbo could resist the temptation of creeping up to the top of Slink's pocket to look at her, though they knew death would be the instant penalty if they were discovered ; and the moment they saw her they both recognised the benevolent Stranger from the Country.

" We have brought you the two little birds you sent us to net, Aunt Spite ; what are we to do with them ? " inquired Giant Slink.

Aunt Spite again.

" Let me peep at their pretty faces," said Aunt Spite, grinning eagerly.

Upon that Slink plunged his hand into his pocket, and pulled out Prince Glee and Tuflongbo, and set them on the supper-table, where their malignant enemy was also standing. She bowed to them derisively, and made them a complimentary speech on the issue of their enterprise, recognising Tuflongbo as the distinguished Traveller, and begging to know from Prince

Glee how a Fairy felt waiting to be married without a bride. This was extremely irritating to their feelings ; but what could they do but endure in patience ? When she had thus mocked them for some time, Giant Slink repeated his inquiry, as to how he was to dispose of his prisoners— the one she had brought, as well us these two fresh ones.

ber
Sug=
gestion,
and " They can all sing ; make lark-pie of them," answered Aunt Spite, and the creasy smiles on her face expanded from ear to ear at the brilliancy of the suggestion. All the Giants, too, roared with laughter, and declared it was a capital idea.

Prince Glee could not put up with this any longer, so he buttoned his coat, and becoming invisible, he flew at Aunt Spite, and tore her cap from her head ; he tweaked her nose, he boxed her ears, he wrung her neck, he pummelled her from one end of the table to the other, and concluded by knocking her head foremost into Giant

Slouchback's dish of soup, where she would
inevitably have been drowned, had not
he, checking the convulsions of mirth
into which her eccentric movements had
thrown him, picked her out, shaken her
dry, and remarking that the old Fairy had
evidently been making too free with the
contents of their cellar, put her up on a
shelf to recover ; whch she did very slowly,
for she was old, and her constitution would
not stand many more such violent assaults.

Tuflongbo had witnessed Prince Glee's
spirited conduct with keen delight ; and
as soon as he unbuttoned his coat and again
stood visible on the supper-table, he inti-
mated his approval and admiration by
significant gestures ; for it was not desirable
to speak at present.

When Aunt Spite had been put up on the
shelf out of the way, the Giants went on
with their supper, and discussed the lark-
pie that was to be made of their prisoners
with greedy gusto ; Tuflongbo reflecting
in his own mind with some satisfaction

**Prince
Glee's
Revenge.**

**Greedy
Old
Giants.**

14

as he listened, that *he*, at all events, should
be a tough morsel, and certain to give
anybody that ate him severe indigestion.
When they had finished, Lumba said,
" Shall we make the pie to-night ? "

" No ; we will make it in the morning ;
I am sleepy," said Slouchback. " Leave
little Trill in her cage, and put these two
pretty birds down in the well where the old
Blackcap is that Slink caught last night.
He shall go into the pie too, for he has a
famous tongue."

And as that was agreed to, Slink took
his luckless prisoners by the small of the
back, and dropped them through a chink in
the floor down, down, down into the dark
bowels of the earth ; and when they recovered the shock of their fall, they found

Down
in the
Well
with
Black-
cap.

themselves in a damp and oozing well,
from which most of the water had drained
away; and an old feeble Fairy, in a black
cap and sable cloak, was sitting there in
the deep silence and solitude, peering so
anxiously through a little hole in the wall,

that he did not notice the arrival of his companions in misfortune, who sat down side by side, and bewailed their dismal fates with bitter anguish.

PRINCE GLEE & TUFLONGBO IN THE GIANTS' WELL, CATCH A GLIMPSE OF THE FACE OF MANNIKIN HOPE

PRINCE GLEE and Tuflongbo had been going on for ever so long in this disconsolate manner before the old Blackcap heard them ; but as soon as he caught the sound of their lamentations, he turned about and questioned them of their names and circumstances. Tuflongbo told him all, and he said he had heard sweet Princess Trill singing mournfully in a cage far overhead ; but as for his making one in the lark-pie, he did not believe it ; for he had just seen the face of Mannikin Hope through the hole in the wall.

He then proposed that the Prince and Tuflongbo should endeavour to catch a glimpse of him too, so the Prince knelt down and applied his eye to the hole. After he had gazed through it earnestly for several minutes, the Blackcap asked him what he saw.

" I see a crowded road, with thousands and thousands of persons all going one way," replied Prince Glee ; " some are running, tripping, stumbling ; some grope as if they were blind ; some have fallen, and do not attempt to rise ; some dance ; a few go leisurely, but directly ; and many saunter as if they knew not whither they are going. But all their eyes look towards the sun-setting, and all have but one end to their journey. Tell me, Blackcap, whither they are all travelling ? "

What Prince Glee saw.

" They are going through Sheneland to Shadowland," replied the Blackcap ; " look amongst those who stumble and grope, and especially amongst those who are fallen, and tell me what thou seest besides."

" I see some person offering them help, and one seems the most in earnest who has a bright, steadfast visage," replied Tuflongbo.

"He of the bright, steadfast visage is Mannikin Hope. Now draw back, to let thy companion behold him too."

So Prince Glee withdrew his eye from the hole in the wall, and Tuflongbo looked through and saw what he had seen.

Hope Stead= fast and True.

" Make your minds easy now," said the Blackcap ; " if you have caught a glimpse of Mannikin Hope, neither you nor Princess Trill will be put into lark-pie. Mannikin Hope is a trustworthy fellow ; he had a fault once, and that was, he thought too much about himself ; but having journeyed through Sheneland to Shadowland, he has learnt wisdom, experience, and unselfish-ness, and now devotes himself solely to the service of others. Shall I tell you his history, to beguile the night ? "

The Prince and Tuflongbo thanked him, and he began as follows :—

Through Sheneland to Shadowland.

" In the Chief City of Sheneland there once dwelt a Cobbler—a crooked little man, with a big head, and buckles to his breeches. Now, for all this Cobbler was little, and crooked, and wore buckles to his breeches, Court fashion, he had a very kind heart, and the poor folks came to him for bread whenever they had nothing to eat in the cupboard at home. And so the reputation of the Cobbler went out to the ends of Sheneland, and he had great fame and favour amongst the Fairies whose country it is.

The Little Old Cobbler, and

" And it happened one day, when the Cobbler was mending shoes, sitting on the bench below his window, he heard a little piping voice in the street outside moaning and saying, ' Here is winter coming, and I have a long way to go—winter is coming, and I have a long way to go ! '

" So the Cobbler got up from his bench, and looking out of the window, espied a boy in thin clothing, without a bit of shoe to his foot, or a bit of cap to his head, and his pretty eyes full of tears.

" When the boy saw the kind Cobbler watching him, he said again even more plaintively than before, ' Winter is coming, and I have a long way to go ! '

" Then cried the Cobbler, ' Come in, my little Mannikin, and rest thee by my fire until the winter is over, and afterwards I will speed thee on thy way.'

" And be sure the little Mannikin came in, nothing loath ; and when he was warmed, the good Cobbler began to ask him of his home and friends.

his En=
quiries.

" ' Whence art thou, little Mannikin ; and who are thy kinsfolk, that have sent thee to travel so far alone ? ' questioned he.

" ' I come from the Country under the Sun, and my kinsfolk are all far ahead of me on the road ; if I do not overtake them by the way, I shall most likely find them at the end of it,' replied Mannikin. 'They have gone through Sheneland to Shadow-land, and I follow.'

" 'I am making that journey myself,' said the Cobbler ; ' but I am drawing near to the close of it now.'

" And all that winter while the snow was on the ground, and the Frost-Elves and Storm-Sprites were working their bitter will over Sheneland, the little Mannikin sat by the Cobbler's fire ; and the Cobbler fed him, and clothed him, and made him a pair of new shoes. When the shoes were finished, the Cobbler set little Mannikin before him, and gave him the following tender advice :—

Making the Shoes.

" 'Thou seest these shoes, Mannikin, that they are square-toed, that the soles are double, and that there are nails in the heels ? If thou takest heed to thy steps, they will last thee all the way thou hast to go, let it be ever so long or ever so rough. And when thou comest to the gates of Shadowland, where thou wilt rejoin thy

kinsfolk, thou must put them off, and leave
them outside. Thou wilt have no further
need of them.'

"And the little Mannikin promised that
he would remember.

"' Listen again, for I have more to say
unto thee,' the Cobbler went on. 'These
shoes are square-toed for Comfort, they
are double-soled for Strength, and they
have nails in the heels for Endurance ; and
thou wilt require them all. And now go ;
make ready thy wallet, for in the morning
thou must begone.'

"Then little Mannikin was very sorrowful at the thought of leaving the good
old Cobbler with the big head and the
buckles to his breeches, and he prayed
him that he might stay with him a little
longer.

"' It cannot be,' replied the Cobbler ;
' Spring is here, and thou hast thy journey
to make. Besides, I am going to my rest.
I have finished my work, and have no
more leather.'

"'But I will call thee in the morning,' said Mannikin.

"'I should not hear thee, though thou call never so loud,' answered the Cobbler. 'By the morning I trust to be safe in Shadowland, for I have been travelling very long, and am right weary.' And with that he turned his face to the wall, and fell asleep.

his Good-night.

"Little Mannikin understood not what the Cobbler meant, but he betook himself woefully to his chamber, and packed his wallet, and set it by the door, ready to start in the morning. And then he sat down by the tired old Cobbler, who had sheltered him though the winter, and fed him, and clothed him, and Mannikin's heart grew so big as he remembered all his kindness that he could not refrain from weeping. He had not wept long, however, when a Tiny Thing hopped upon his foot, and cried cheerfully, 'On with thy shoes, Mannikin — the new shoes, square-toed, double-soled, and with nails in the heels ;

for the sun is coming up, and it is time to be setting off on thy journey. The Gate of Youth has been open since the dawning, and thou hast had leisure enough to make ready.'

Cobbler
—Till we
meet
again.

" So little Mannikin gently touched the Cobbler, to make him say Good-bye; but the Tiny Thing hopped upon his hand, and plucked it hastily away.

" ' Let him rest,' whispered she; ' did he not tell thee that he had finished his work, and had no more leather ? '

" But Mannikin still lingered, and his sobs and cries filled the house : ' He will not hear thee, though thou lament never so loud,' said Tiny Thing gently. ' Be comforted, Mannikin ; he has reached the quiet rest of Shadowland, and thou wilt find him there with thy kinsfolk when thou reachest thy journey's end.'

" Then Mannikin, with one last look at his kind old benefactor, put on his shoes, slung his wallet on his back, and went out of the house, the door of which instantly

closed behind him. In his grief and haste
he had shaken off the Tiny Thing, but he
had not gone many paces when he heard
her calling after him : ' Carry me with
thee, Mannikin—carry me with thee.' So
he waited a moment until she overtook
him and hopped upon his shoulder.

" ' Thou art no great weight,' said he,
caressing her.

" ' I shall bear the half of all *thy* burdens,'
was Tiny Thing's answer. ' Thou wilt
travel much more lightly with me than if
thou wert to leave me behind. For I am
Cheerfulness, and I am good company for
wayfarers through Sheneland to Shadowland, whether they be young or old, rich
or poor. Mind, therefore, Mannikin, that
thou lose me not.'

" And so they went through the streets
of the city from the Cobbler's House ; no
man taking any heed to them ; and Tiny
Thing singing like a bird in Mannikin's ear—

'Mannikin, be of good cheer, good cheer,
Mannikin, be of good cheer !'

"Then she changed her note, and sung—

'A merry heart goes all the way,
And lightens the longest and darkest day;
Mannikin, be of good cheer, good cheer,
Mannikin, be of good cheer!'

"And Mannikin, though he never forgot the kind old Cobbler with the big head, and the buckles to his breeches, began to remember him with less sadness; and when he reached the gates of the City, there was such a press of young men and maidens going out like himself upon their journey, that he had quite enough to do to take care of his wallet, and of Tiny Thing on his shoulder, without thinking at all.

"Everybody seemed to be in haste, and Mannikin caught the infection of their hurry. Throughout the morning he pushed on with the crowd, tripping, stumbling, bruising himself, and missing many a beautiful sight which he might just as well have enjoyed. He gave no help to any who were less strong than himself, and hardly

heard the offers of kindness and companionship that were made to him, for he was
thinking peevishly what a long way he had
to go, and distressing himself in vain by
previsions of all the ills that might befall
him ere he reached his journey's end.
Tiny Thing had to sing in his ear again and
again to warn him—

> 'Fairly and Softly went far in a day,
> Hurry and Hotfoot soon lost their way!'

" And then Mannikin would slacken his
speed, and take rather more heed to where
he set his feet ; but though by noon he was
much wearied and heated, he never thought
of sitting down to rest, and consider his
doings, until there overtook him an old
Greybeard, who said to him kindly,
' Whither away so fast, Mannikin ? '

Hope on, hope ever.

" ' To Shadowland, father,' replied
Mannikin.

" ' Thou wilt reach it none the sooner
for thy haste,' said the Greybeard solemnly.
' Take thy time, or thou wilt have many

false steps to recover, and false ways to retrace. Sit here and listen to the voices in the air a little while——'

" ' They can teach me nothing. I have a long way to go ; I pray thee keep me not,' pleaded Mannikin.

" But the Tiny Thing whispered in his ear, ' Most haste, worst speed, Mannikin. Hearken to Greybeard, and rest. I have felt thee limping twice already. Is there not a sharp stone in thy shoe ? '

" Now, Mannikin had felt a pebble galling his heel for some miles back, but he had hardly thought it worth while to wait to take it out ; at Tiny Thing's bidding, however, he plucked off his shoe, sought it, and flung it away. Meanwhile, the Greybeard questioned him of his journey ; whence he had started ; whom he had met by the way ; what he had done, and what he had seen.

" ' I started from the house of the old Cobbler with the big head, and buckles to his breeches. He had finished his work

Most
haste,
worst
Speed.

and had no more leather, and in his sleep he passed away to the rest of Shadow-land.'

" 'I knew the Cobbler,' said the Grey-beard. 'He was a friend of mine, and my most honest counsellor.'

" 'He was a friend of mine, too,' added Mannikin. 'He sheltered, clothed, and fed me ; and when I was to set off on my journey, he gave me these excellent shoes.'

" 'The best gift he could have given thee,' replied Greybeard. 'I am glad that thou hast talked with Gratitude and Thankfulness about him, for that is good for thy conscience. Never-forget is the salt of all benefits, Mannikin, and see that thou keep good store of it. But, except Tiny Thing on thy shoulder, thou hast no companion. How is that ? Hast thou out-walked the crowds who thronged thee early in the morning ? Did none offer thee their fellowship ? '

" 'I saw some who would fain have joined me, but they proceeded so slowly,

Never-forget is the Salt of all Benefits.

15

I soon left them behind. I remembered that I had a long way to go.'

" ' So have they, Mannikin, and thou shouldst have helped some of the weak ones along with thee. It would have lost thee no time. What were their names whom thou leftest behind upon the road ? '

" ' There was Careful, who never stepped unless he were sure to step on solid ground, and though he came out this morning from the City-gate with myself, he had hardly a speck on his shoes ; but I came straight on, and sometimes the path was very miry.'

" ' So I see,' said the Greybeard. " O Mannikin, those beclogged shoes of thine will be lead to thy feet before thou reachest Shadowland, unless Good-deeds will set about rubbing off some of the mire. But whom didst thou pass besides Careful ? '

" ' I passed Brotherly Kindness and Charity, helping some sick folk who were cast out of a city where there was the plague. They called to me to lend a hand, but I told them I had still a long way to go, and that if they wished to get to Shadowland by nightfall, they had better mind their own business and come along.'

" ' O Mannikin, short-sighted art thou ! They were good angels from Shadowland, sent thence, in company with Mercy, to help all who fall into trouble. Thou shouldst have joined thyself to them. And who besides these didst thou pass upon the road ? '

Hope's Short-sightedness.

" ' I saw Friendship, but I told him I wanted no help ; and Love with a bleeding heart, but I had not time to bind her wounds ; and Avarice, who went a little way with me, and then dropped behind ; and Confidence, whom I trusted, and who got me the worst fall I have had yet ; and Knavery, who first deceived and then beat me : and now it is noon and I am growing faint, though I have still a long way to go.'

" ' So thou hast, Mannikin, and a dreary, seeing thou hast chosen to leave those behind who would have been pleasant company. If thou hadst taken Friendship by the hand, he would never have left thee; and if thou hadst dressed the wounds of Love, she would never have failed thee of comfort.'

" ' I have just seen one companion who, I think, would suit me,' said Mannikin.

" ' What is his name ? ' asked the Greybeard.

" ' Self-Help,' replied Mannikin.

Tbe Sbort= comings of Self= belp. " ' A presumptuous, conceited fellow is Self-Help, though his company is better than none,' said Greybeard ; ' but I warn thee, Mannikin, that he will put thee on doing many things without either honour or profit ; and when thou hast accomplished them, he will be the first to sneer and ask thee what good they are of. I wish that thou hadst taken Love and Friendship instead, for the sun grows hot in the afternoon, and there are many dark and dangerous places before thee. Thou hast not done well, but thou hast done according to thy light ; so now I will wish thee good speed. I blame thee not ; but remember, after Experience has spoken with thee, thy conscience must bear the follies of the time future.' And so the Greybeard went on his way, and the little Mannikin on his ; and Mannikin felt sadder at heart even than he had done when the old Cobbler turned his face to the wall and fell asleep, because he had finished his work and had no more leather.

Nothing like Experience.

" Tiny Thing peeped round and beheld his sorrowful countenance, and it subdued her so much, that for ever so long she had no heart to sing ; but at last she began very softly, as if trying how he would take it—

> 'Past is the past, Mannikin, past is the past,
>   Thou canst not undo it;
> Work thy best from first to last,
>   And thou wilt never rue it.
> Wisdom comes with wisdom teeth,
>   Experience with grey hair;
> Self-help a lusty helper is,
>   And I'll stave off dull Care.'

Tiny Thing comforts Hope.

And to Tiny Thing's great satisfaction, his

visage cleared again, and he called, in a manful voice, for his new comrade to come up and walk along beside him. So Self-Help advanced, making loud professions, and looking very stout and determined; and they trudged on abreast until they came to a wide open common, where many roads crossed like a network of chalky lines amongst heather and furze-bushes. There was nothing to shelter them from the glowing heat, and Self-Help by and by turned sick and faint, and wanted to go

Self-help fails.

back; but Mannikin said, No, there could be no going back, and they kept on for a long while, never making much progress, however, for they got confused in the maze of roads, and without being aware of it, returned again and again on their steps. Twice they had passed some great gray stones, from below which gushed and gurgled a little spring, whose sparkling waters had worn themselves a channel in the moor, and went singing on their way without ever ceasing, though the sun was

hot enough to dry up even the rivers in the
lowlands. Mannikin took off his shoes,
and laved his feet in the cool water, for
they were very much swollen, and painful
in the extreme ; and while he did it, Self-
Help, who had been the real cause of his
going by all these roundabout ways, which
led nowhere, sat behind him in the sulks,
scolding and chafing mightily. Mannikin
tried not to listen ; but he could not shut
his ears, and he was forced to hear himself
called by many hard names, which were
most of them true. Self-Help remembered,
now that it was too late, that he might have
taken counsel with Forethought about
these new regions which he had never
travelled before ; but rather than acknowledge that his conceited presumption had
been his false and wearisome guide, he
preferred to seek a scapegoat on whom to
lay the blame, and told Mannikin pettishly
that it was all his fault.

Self-
help
sulks.

" Mannikin was much annoyed, and
would very likely have given way to anger

himself, had not Tiny Thing begun to sing, in her soft, cooing tone—

'Patience, Mannikin, wait awhile,
    Who is this that cometh?
Peace in her sweet eyes,
    Faith in her grave smile,
Who is this that cometh?
    Meet her, Mannikin, arise, arise!'

and looking down by the watercourse, he saw advancing towards him a fair woman, with a frank front and great beauty of face.

"'Who art thou?' asked Mannikin, regarding her tender countenance very wistfully.

"'I am Affection, the younger sister of Love,' said she.

"'If thou art going my way, come with me,' Mannikin besought her.

"'Why didst not thou take Love for a companion? I know thou didst meet with her early in the morning,' said Affection, with tender reproach.

"'I met her, but she was sorely wounded; her very heart bled, and I thought I had

I have
so far to
go—I
have so
far to go.

not time to bind up her wounds, for I had then a long way to go. Canst thou tell me if she is healed? She had a face like heaven: it haunts my dreams day and night. Scarcely knew I how fair she was until I had left her; and then, though I sought her carefully, sought her with bitter tears, never have I found her again—never since I started on my journey have I found anything so beautiful as the morning face of Love, as I first met her in the sunny lanes of Youth. It was a cruel hand that struck her. O Love, Love!'

"'She is dead, Mannikin; lament is vain. Thou wilt see her no more until thou enterest into Shadowland, where all things are forgotten. But give me thy hand. I will help thee as well as I can, though I am neither so strong nor so patient as my sister was.'

"Then sang Tiny Thing in Mannikin's ear—

> 'Love was lovelier, Mannikin,
> Love was lovelier far:

Love lost.

Love is best.

But hold Affection fast, for she is good
And helpful where life's darkest passes are.'

" And so Mannikin, Affection, Self-Help,
and Tiny Thing went on their way again.
For some time they kept by the pleasant
watercourse, where the sun had less power,
because of the breeze from the water ; and
presently the heat began to decline, and
the shadows to deepen and lengthen, until,
when they came to the outskirts of a great
forest, it seemed that the twilight had
suddenly fallen. Mannikin began to fear
that they had lost the track once more,
but Affection gently reassured him.

" ' It is the approach of evening, but we
are on the right road, Mannikin,' said she.
' There is not far to go now, for already
we are on the borders of Shadowland.'

Nearing
Shadow=
land.

" To hear this cheered Mannikin exceedingly ; for it seemed a weary while
since the poor old Cobbler, with the big
head, and buckles to his breeches, had set
him off on his journey, and gone to sleep
himself, because he had finished his work

and had no more leather. Tiny Thing was very tired too, and chirped so feebly now that he could scarcely hear her ; and Self-Help lagged often, and was near fainting by the time they came out of the wood at the other side : but Affection still held him by the hand, and when he complained of his fatigue or of the weight of his wallet, which galled his shoulders, she bade him look up. And when Mannikin looked up, he saw before him a range of lofty hills hung over with mists and vapours of darkness, but overhead the star-lamps of Shadowland shone faintly through the clouds.

Star-lamps in View.

" ' Leave here thy wallet, Mannikin ; thou canst not climb the hill with that on thy back,' whispered Affection ; but Self-Help urged him to carry it farther, and he struggled hard to do so, but could make no way at all ; and at last he said, ' Take it off, take it off ; it is only stones ; ' and Affection loosed the bands, and it was left at the wayside. When Mannikin began to mount the hill, he found that from his shoes he had lost half the soles of Strength, that the square toes of Comfort were broken into holes, and that most of the nails of Endurance had fallen out; but Affection led him by the easiest places, and encouraged him with many good words.

The Shoes last their time.

"And at last he heard a strange voice speaking, which said, 'Mannikin, put off thy shoes; they are worn out, and thou hast done with them.'

"Then the warm clasp of Affection was loosed from his hand, and he was suddenly enwrapped in the dark mist wreaths, and all the perils and sufferings of his journey through Sheneland were forgotten. And he was alone. Affection stood weeping below the cloud; Self-Help had dropped down beside the wallet of stones; and the last he heard of Tiny Thing was her little voice singing farewell to him far away in the distance.

"And all at once he was in Shadowland, and there was the old Cobbler with the big head, and the buckles to his breeches, and his kinsfolk who had arrived before him, waiting to welcome him.

" ' Thou art here sooner than I expected, Mannikin,' said the good Cobbler. ' I had many fears for thee, when I heard that thou hadst left behind thee Charity and Brotherly Kindness, Love and Friendship. Who were thy guides, since thou wouldst none of them ? '

The Cobbler's Welcome.

" ' I chose Cheerfulness, Self-Help, and Affection,' replied Mannikin.

" ' Thou mightest have chosen better ; but since thou hast made thy journey, thou must needs want rest. Did my shoes wear well ? '

" ' They lasted me until I came to the verge of Shadowland, and the One Invisible bade me put them off, for I had done with them.'

" ' As they wore well, they must have been made of sound leather. Many poor travellers stumble and hurt themselves, because they have started on their journey without shoes, or shod only with some poor stuff, which soon drops into rags amongst the stones and thorns. It is amongst such poor, barefooted, crippled travellers that Charity and Mercy find so much work to do. Thou shouldst have thought less of thyself, Mannikin, and have gone to help them. The saddest and most wearied of wayfarers goes on his way rejoicing, when he sees the face of *Hope*.'

Mannikin Hope

" ' I will return. Send me now, for I am ready,' cried Mannikin penitently.

" And the old Cobbler took him at his word, and suffered him to go back into Sheneland, to do his neglected work. And that is why, in the darkest abodes of Sheneland, and in the roughest roads by which men, as they go to the solemn Shadowland, must journey, Hope is always to be met, with a steadfast face, waiting on Mercy and Charity, and sometimes stretching forth a hand and helping those poor creatures who may never be found out even by them. For Hope has made

the journey himself, and he remembers his shelter in the Cobbler's house through the winter, and what a long way he had to go when he left it ; and he knows that he can cheer the faintest and weakest on the weary road.

Cheers the faint.

" And so he does ; for there are now few homes so dark that he cannot brighten them, and few hearts so heavy that they have not a welcome for Mannikin Hope, the faithfullest guide of travellers through Sheneland to Shadowland."

When the excellent old Blackcap had finished his story, he was almost fainting with thirst ; so Prince Glee kindly gave him the golden olive to suck, and he and Tuflongbo both tasted it too, and were marvellously refreshed ; after which, the Prince restored it carefully to his knapsack.

It was now getting towards morning, and the three captives down in the well naturally began to feel very anxious as to their fate. Tuflongbo kept himself the easiest, for he was a philosopher, and found distraction in watching and speculating upon the strange multitudes whom he saw through the hole in the wall hurrying along the road through Sheneland to Shadowland.

"What a worry and fuss they make over trifles," cried he, in grieved amazement; "and, at the same time, what golden opportunities for good do they pass by, as if they were nought! How the empty pates go tip-toeing along in serene self-complacency till they fall into a bog, and how some of the worthiest go limping in the ruts. It is a queer way this, a very queer way through Sheneland to Shadowland!"

At this point, Tuflongbo's philosophic meditations were cut short by Giant Slink roaring out from above, "You three little birds down there, fly up and be made lark-pie of!" And thrusting his great hand through the chink of the floor down into the well, they were obliged to hop upon his outstretched perches of fingers,

Lark-
pie.

and so were lifted up into the cavern where the Giants had supped the night before. Slink then pinioned them, and put them into the pie-dish all in a row, and told them to sit there quietly until he brought the other lark that was to go into the pie with them. Tuflongbo whispered that he was afraid it was all up with them now; but Prince Glee could only think of his approaching reunion with Princess Trill. Mournful as the circumstances would undoubtedly be, he felt in his own mind that it would be happier to be made into a lark-pie with her than to be separated *for ever*, and he knew that she would think the same. As for the Blackcap, he said nothing, for he was still out of breath with telling that long story down in the well.

HOW the GIANTS CHANGED their MIND ABOUT MAKING LARK-PIE of PRINCESS TRILL, PRINCE GLEE, TUFLONGBO & the BLACKCAP, & WHAT THEY DID WITH THEM AFTERWARDS

WHEN Giant Slink left Prince Glee, Tuflongbo, and the Blackcap, sitting in the pie-dish all in a row, he went out of his cavern and straight along under a gloomy wall until he came to a sudden turning and heard a perfect flood of the most delicious melody swelling out upon the air. Passing round the corner, he looked up and saw Princess Trill in her cage, pouring out her heart in a song, sweet and full as a choir of nightingales, while Giant Slouchback and Giant Lumba

242

sat on the ground below, listening to her with open-mouthed surprise, their big hands embracing their big knees, and their eyes staring with rapt admiration. Giant Slink was almost paralysed with wonder, but he dropped down on a stone beside his brother Giants, and listened too.

Princess Trill now showed her own lovely face, for Aunt Spite had economically reflected that as she was returning to Sheneland she might as well take her Mask with her, where, perhaps, she might sell it at half-price ; this was the first time the Giants had seen the Princess without the Mask, and the effect her beauty had upon them was very remarkable. Not until after they had listened to her sweet singing three days and three nights, did they remember their other prisoners, whom they had left sitting in the pie-dish all in a row, and Slouchback proposed that they should be brought and made to sing too. So Slink went back to the cavern, and returned with the pie-dish under his arm. Then Lumba,

Princess Trill shows her face.

who was by far the most good-natured of the Giants, took Princess Trill out of her cage and set her on his hand, and Prince Glee beside her, and when they flew into each other's arms and rapturously embraced, he declared they were such a pretty little pair it was a shame to separate them ; and with that he put them back into the cage together, and the two began to sing such a transporting song that the three Giants were almost crazy with delight.

Re-union.

Meanwhile Tuflongbo and Blackcap had also been caged together, and when Princess Trill and Prince Glee ceased singing they began to chatter, and, if truth must be told, to quarrel too, as learned friends will ; for Tuflongbo now discovered that Blackcap was a stray member of the Royal Society of Wiseacres of Sheneland, whose specialty was ancient history and mythology, and they were naturally jealous of each other's distinction. The Giants listened a little while to them also, and then Lumba said, " These are talking

The
Giants
en=
tranced
with
Princess
Trill's
Singing.

ALL·THEIR·EYES ⨯⨯
STARING·WITH·RAPT
ADMIRATION ⨯⨯⨯

birds ; we will keep them too ; they will be
great fun ; and Aunt Spite will never
know. She must be half-way through
Rockpass by this time, and there are
birds enough to be caught without making
lark-pie of such clever birds as these.''

And his brother Giants agreed with him,
and the poor captives all began to sing
together in exultation at their reprieve
in a way even more bewitching and bewildering than before. All Wildwaste
echoed with the melody, and other Giants
came trooping from far and near over
the hills, and sat down circle beyond circle
round the cages, with their big hands
clasping their big knees and all their eyes
staring with rapt admiration at lovely
Princess Trill in her robes of gossamer,
silver, and wild white roses, and Prince
Glee in his smart wedding clothes and the
Magic Button on his coat. It was a very
wonderful and imposing scene, as beheld
from Tuflongbo's cage, and he took particular note of all the details, that he might

**Giants
at a
Concert.**

be able to give a flourishing account of it to the Fairy Queen and her Court whenever he and his fellow-captives escaped from the dreadful Country of the Giants and returned to Sheneland.

Now, unfortunately, the Giants were rather quarrelsome fellows amongst themselves, and when they had had singing enough, they got upon their feet and began to fight, probably for amusement and variety, but very much, nevertheless, to the terror of Princess Trill. Prince Glee took the utmost pains to reassure her, and said it was a magnificent spectacle— he had never expected to see a Battle of the Giants ; but she trembled all over, and wept for fear. Meanwhile, all the vast plain of Wildwaste quaked under the rush and stamping of their heavy feet ; their hoarse cries resounded like shocks of thunder, and their ponderous blows fell like sledge-hammers on each other's bones. Tuflongbo was in ecstasy. He sat down on the floor of his cage, and clapped his

A Battle
of
Giants.

hands; he cheered the Giants on with shrill cries of approbation and promises of how he would glorify their mighty deeds in his next volume of travels; but the feeble old Blackcap groaned and sighed, and said, " Oh! how he wished he were in his peaceful study in sunny, quiet Sheneland! Could not the Giants settle their differences with their tongues as Wiseacres did ? "

The Giants having once begun to fight never ceased until it became dark, and by that time the ground was covered with their wounded; but in the dead of the night they all contrived to creep away, without the poor caged captives being aware of it: and when the morning broke there was nobody in sight but Slouchback, Slink, and Lumba, who had fallen asleep under the wall, and were snoring horribly.

Dark=ness ends the Fight.

" I wish these lazy fellows would wake up," said Tuflongbo impatiently; " I see no fun in staying here, and, besides, I am hungry."

Prince Glee, overhearing that, passed the Golden Olive round, and everybody was much refreshed thereby ; so much so, that Princess Trill herself proposed that they should rouse their mighty jailers with a morning song. And they all began and went on until first one of the big fellows and then another opened his eyes, yawned, stretched himself, and staggered upon his feet in anything but a pleasant temper.

A Morning Song.

" It is the little birds ! " grumbled Slouchback ; " what a row they make ! Slink, you had better put them down the well again, I can't stand this ; or else go and make lark-pie of them, as Aunt Spite said."

" Nay, nay, I have a better thought than that," replied Slink ; " you remember that old bird-fancier who lost his way in Rockpass last year ? I'll carry them over the mountains, and sell them to him. He is always seeking new birds to sing in Elfin Wood."

" But Aunt Spite will find it out, and

say we have broken our agreement,"
suggested Lumba.

" Who cares for Aunt Spite ? I wish we
had made crow-pie of *her* ; for, would you
believe it, Slouchback ? she gave us Bad
Money," said Slink.

" Bad Money ! " roared Slouchback.
" Ah ! that comes of dealing with anybody
who wears the Mask of Pious Hypocrisy."

" If I knew what would vex her most,
I'd set about doing it directly ! " cried
Lumba ; " the double-faced old cheat ! "

And so said all the Giants, and then they
sat in a ring on the ground, sulkily con-
templating the three brass tokens Aunt
Spite had passed off upon them for genuine
money. The Captives had heard their
discourse with lively interest ; and hardly
could Tuflongbo restrain himself from
making suggestions of revenge to them,
but Prince Glee signed to him authori-
tatively to hold his tongue and go on
listening.

And presently Slouchback took up one

Crow-
pie.

brass token, and Slink took up another, and Lumba took up the third, and they spun them through the air over the farthest range of black mountains, and where they fell they became stagnant lakes in the Water-World. After that they got up, and Slouchback said, " I wonder what would vex Aunt Spite most," in such an anxiously reflective tone, that Tuflongbo could no longer keep himself from breaking forth into the wildest suggestions. He said, " Hang her; give her to the Wicked Fairy of the Creeping Plant with many Tendrils ; lock her up in her own ancestral mansion of Castle Craft ; hand her over to Clutch in the Enclosed Garden on the borders of Sheneland, where the sun never shines ; let Quip, Crank, and Wink have the custody of her in the Royal Lock-up ;" but Giant Lumba interrupted him with the reminder that they had not got Aunt Spite there, and so could not put her through any of these penalties ; on which, Tuflongbo lapsed into a very depressed state of mind, from which he was only roused by hearing Prince Glee say, in a cheerful tone, " I know what would vex Aunt Spite most,—it would vex her most to see Princess Trill and me married, and living happily ever afterwards ! "

On hearing that all the Giants sprang upon their legs, seized the cages, and set off at a famous swinging trot towards Rockpass. Arrived there, they opened the doors, and freed their prisoners, bidding them creep through and make haste, and go and vex Aunt Spite to the utmost. So Prince Glee and Princess Trill, and Tuflongbo and the Blackcap took their leave of the amiable Giants ; but before they went Tuflongbo begged to inquire if there was anything he could do for them in Sheneland, but as they are dull fellows, and not quick at imagining, they only rubbed their heads and said, " No, they did not know there was."

Liberty.

" But I say, Old Fellow, do you know the taste of fruit of Aplepivi ? " asked the Traveller, with winning familiarity. " Do you know the flavour of Golden Honey of Puffrasp and Alicompane ?—you *don't*? Then I'll give you a treat. Come here to-morrow at this time—neither earlier nor later—and here you will find three carpet-bags stuffed with those delicious commodities. And when you have once tasted them, you'll remember Tuflongbo, your benefactor, as long as you live."

And when he had said this, he slipped into Rockpass after his companions, and in a very few minutes they had got through, and were speeding merrily on towards the Enchanted Bower, hardly able to believe that it was true, and that they had really been permitted to depart unharmed out of the awful Country of the Giants.

The RETURN of PRINCE GLEE PRINCESS TRILL, TUFLONGBO & THE BLACKCAP TO ELFIN COURT

WHEN the four escaped prisoners reached the Enchanted Bower, all the Fairy-bells throughout Sheneland began to ring their loudest and fastest.

Her Majesty was at dinner at the moment, but immediately she rose up and commanded a Royal Procession to go out and meet the Prince and Princess.

" There will be a Wedding to-day, and let everyone be ready," said she ; and as soon as the Grand Pomp had marshalled

Back to
Elfin
Court.

253

his Heralds, Banner-bearers of poppy silk,
and Trumpeters, all the Court poured
forth and fell into the procession, the
Queen herself going first on her white
butterfly, and the miscellaneous crowd of
Royal officials bringing up the rear. Mother
Dignity was in a dreadful flutter, and
Worry and Dopple were wild with joy as
they scampered off in advance of everybody, and presently they came to the
house made in the hollow trunk of the
Ash-Tree, where lived Old Woman and
her little Maid Brisk. They were hard at
work, as usual, but at the Queen's command the procession paused, and her
Majesty asked—

" Have you seen Prince Glee and Princess
Trill pass by this way ? "

" No, but they are coming, Fairy Queen,
they are coming, and Tuflongbo and an
old Blackcap with them," replied Old
Woman.

Then the Royal Procession moved on
again, and stopped next where poor little

Fairy
Queen
going
first on
her
White
Butter=
fly.

Idle lay amongst the nettles, with the Wicked Fairy of the Creeping Plant with many Tendrils keeping guard over her. Her Majesty looked down at the unhappy prisoner, and asked again, " Have you seen Prince Glee and Princess Trill pass by this way ? " and Idle answered, " No, Fairy Queen, but they are close at hand, with Tuflongbo and a Blackcap."

And directly afterwards the returned prisoners and the Royal Procession met.

Then Fairy Queen descended from her butterfly, and embraced sweet Princess Trill and her Cousin Prince Glee, and com- **A Royal Greeting.** manded the Knights-Fairy to form double lines on either side of them that they might be conveyed safely back to Elfin Court. The Queen and Princess Trill went first, and by the way the Princess related to her Royal Mistress what had befallen her since she was carried away by her Aunt Spite in the Mask of Pious Hypocrisy. And Prince Glee followed behind with Prince Goldheart, and told his adventures; and

Tuflongbo told his, and made the most of them, and the Blackcap said to his brother Wiseacres that what had happened to him elucidated certain mysteries of the ancients, and that he would make them a solid quarto volume about it in the course of the next hundred years.

And when the Royal Procession reached the Palace the whole Court passed straight into the Grand Hall, which was crowded in every corner to see the Wedding of Prince Glee and Princess Trill, who advanced with her Majesty and went up the steps of the Daïs of Beauty. The Fairy-bells were ringing rejoicingly all the time, and everybody said to his neighbour that it was a most inspiriting event.

Then the Queen placed the Prince and Princess one on each side of her footstool, and bade them join hands, and Mother Dignity fussed about the sweet bride, and covered her with the veil of silver gossamer, after which the Grand Pomp ordered a blast of trumpets, and Muffin, Master of

the Ceremonies, proclaimed silence. Then rose Fairy Queen from her Golden Throne, and with Serene Majesty, spoke as follows:—

" These are our beloved Cousins, Prince Glee and Princess Trill, who have escaped the persecutions of their enemies and the perils of Wildwaste. They now profess their mutual love and affection in the presence of Elfin Court, and who shall *dare* to say them *Nay* ? "

And then her Majesty paused and looked round, and saw, standing on the Stool of Penance, where Catch and Keep had placed her, the benevolent Stranger from the Country, who had been brought to Court to witness festivities, but this time against her will. Fancy, the Court Moralist and Story-Teller, and Stern-visaged Truth, were standing near her, and at the Royal Address her broad face full of creases of smiles was seen to quiver like jelly. But she dared not accept the challenge, or deny the love of the Prince and Princess. She knew that her day was over for good, and that

17

they would be married now in defiance of all her machinations. And as nobody spoke, her gracious Majesty continued—

An Invitation to mate.

" If there be any more true lovers in this my Court who would now desire to betroth themselves in the presence of this dignified assemblage, let them approach the Daïs and stand before my footstool below Prince Glee and Princess Trill."

At that announcement, a thrill of joy and surprise ran through half the Fairies present, and immediately there was a good deal of whispering, and blushing, and coaxing, and nonsense—all which her Majesty tolerated with infinite patience for some time ; but at length it became tedious, and she remarked to Muffin that, as it seemed

Bashful Fairies

no one else was going to be married that day besides the Prince and Princess, perhaps they had better proceed. But no sooner had she spoken than there was a general commotion and movement towards the Daïs of Beauty, and a great flutter amongst the Maids of Honour and Royal Pages.

The candidates for betrothal now pressed forward so fast that Muffin had more than enough to do to marshal them in pairs ; but when the task was accomplished, and the Queen looked round upon the youth and beauty of her Court, kneeling before her, she saw that Frolic and Clipsome had joined hands, that Dump and Touchy had done likewise ; that Wink had got little Dot ; that Tippety Wichet and his Brothers had chosen the lovely sister Elves, Posy, Dove, and Poppet ; that Trip, Try-for-it, Finick, Turn, Twist, Lush, and Trap were proposing to mate themselves with Blue-Bell, Satin, Sleek, Sly, Flip, Arch, and Dimple ; and that Tippet was hunting about for a bride, and getting himself refused by everybody. The last to approach the Daïs were Snip, Snap, and Snarl, who had been judiciously selected by the sour Professors, Birch, Cane, and Ferule, who looked very much satisfied with their choice. They rather spoilt the effect of the group of youth and beauty clustered

Make up their minds.

round the Throne, but her Majesty courteously accepted their promises, and they were married along with the rest.

Sour Grapes. Then Tippet, being left to himself below, whispered to a friend that, for *his* part, he was sure the bachelors had the best of it in the long run, and that he was thankful to have escaped the snares of the young Court beauties; and his friend replied, "No doubt of it." He knew the taste of sour grapes himself, and quite agreed with Tippet.

And when the august ceremony was over, there was a general murmur of satisfaction; all the blessed pairs stood up, hand in hand, smiling and blushing, and looking as proud and as bright as May-day; but Prince Glee and Princess Trill looked happier and lovelier than any of the rest, and at the provoking spectacle the benevolent Stranger from the Country opened her mouth and gave utterance to a screeching yell of rage, which rang from one end of the Palace to the other. At this startling breach of

Court Etiquette, Fancy gave the signal, and immediately Truth raised his hand and plucked the Mask of Pious Hypocrisy from her face, and behold it was *Aunt Spite*.

The Mask plucked off.

Then orders were given to remove the prisoner, and she was shut up in a dark van, where her friends, Slander, Mischief, Gossip, Idlewords, Wrinkle, Whisper, Sneer, and Twaddle, had already been secured, and they were all carted off to the Enclosed Garden on the borders of Sheneland where the Sun never shines ; where they were presently joined by Pickle, Prig, and Slumph, and the Wicked Fairy of the Creeping Plant with many Tendrils, who had been commanded to set little Idle free, on account of the information she had given to Prince Glee and Tuflongbo when they were setting out in pursuit of Princess Trill. She afterwards took service with Professor Birch's wife, and has unlearnt many of her lazy ways.

After these obnoxious characters had been got rid of, Fairy Queen issued her

**happy
ever
after.** Royal Mandate that everybody should be
happy ; so they adjourned to the Hall of
Dancing, and there was a magnificent Ball,
which went on until there was a magnificent
Supper ; after which all the company danced
again, till they had hardly a leg to stand on.

And the wedding festivities were kept
up for six weeks, with Plays, Pantomimes,
Magic Lanterns, Conjurers, Tumblers,
Stories, Games, Entertainments, and all
manner of Delightful Recreations.

And the anniversary of the Wedding Day
is kept still as one of the most distinguished
festivals in Sheneland, and Prince Glee and
Princess Trill lived happily ever afterwards.

THE GREEN SHOES

By EFFIE H. FREEMANTLE

THE GREEN SHOES.

HUNDREDS and hundreds of years ago there lived in a cottage on the borders of Tanglewood a little old woman who always sat at her door spinning, spinning, spinning. A long time ago she had been quite four feet high, but from long bending over her spinning-wheel she had shrunk and shrunk until she was scarcely three feet high.

Now, the most remarkable thing about this little old woman was that she always wore a pair of bright green shoes ; rain or shine, it did not matter which, you would see her at her doorway with her two little feet encased in the green shoes.

Nearly half a mile away from the little old woman's cottage there lived a good farmer and his wife, who had one little daughter named Marigold ; they called her so because God had sent her to them when all the marigolds were blooming in their garden. At the time of which I am writing she was just eight years old, and her parents were very proud of her, for she was a tall, slim little maiden. She had, however, one great fault—she was very wilful ; and often when they told her, in their anxiety for her welfare, not to go through Tanglewood—as soon as she got outside the house, by herself, she would stamp one little foot and be very angry—because she did not understand their care for her, and she wanted to go through Tanglewood.

So it happened that one day when she was standing on its borders, near to where Old Woman's cottage was, she spied her sitting at her door, sitting as usual with her feet encased in the green shoes, perched upon a little stool. So she ran up to her and said—

" Little old woman, why do you always

wear those bright green shoes ? " and
the old woman said, " Maiden, I wear
them because they are magic shoes that
a fairy gave to me long ago, and every
day, so long as you wear them, you can
have one wish that shall be granted to
you."

" Then why," said Marigold, " since
you can have that wish, do you not live
in a great big golden palace instead of
sitting in a cottage spinning flax all day ? "

But the tiny old woman looked at her
very gravely for a minute, and then she
said—

" Little maiden, I tried the palaces
years ago, and now I know that flax is
best for me."

And Marigold stamped her little foot
again, and said, " Oh, lend me the shoes !
lend me the shoes !   I don't believe you ! "

And the little old woman, with a half-
sad smile, handed her the shoes, and said,
" Try."

Marigold put them on—you see they

**Won't
Believe
Work is
best.**

fitted her because the little old woman was so small that her feet were just as tiny as Marigold's own. She ran out of the cottage quite forgetting to say " Thank you," and stood for a moment looking at her beloved Tanglewood. Then, not remembering the green shoes, she said to herself—

Green Shoes for Wishes.

" How I wish I could get to the other end of Tanglewood, and that mother and father would not worry or think about me at all ! "

And lo and behold ! everything went dark for a minute, and she found herself at the other end of Tanglewood. She knew then that she had had a wish, and that it had been granted. She felt very miserable and lonely, and, after all, there was nothing at the end of Tanglewood, except a few tall pine trees that swayed and swished in the cold twilight like tall ghosts, and frightened her terribly ; however, being a brave little maiden, she started to make the best of her way home.

It was a very long way, and very dark in Tanglewood ; and, worst of all, there started a drizzling rain which made her very cold and her frock so heavy with the damp that it was nearly midnight before she got to the door of the farmhouse. To her surprise, there was no light in any of the windows, and no anxious mother or father seeking for her.

She had to knock a very long while before her mother came to the door, and when she opened it Marigold was surprised to hear her say, in quite a calm voice, " Oh, here you are ! Run upstairs to bed ! "

There was no nice warm bread-and-milk, no loving arms put out to clasp her safe and sound—only a cold little bed waiting for her, and no one to attend to it. Her mother had gone. It was then she re-remembered that part of her wish, that mother and father wouldn't worry about her. She cried herself to sleep, and in the middle of her tears she said to herself—

" To-morrow I'll be sensible, and have a

Unwise Wishes.

really nice wish." Then I think she fell asleep.

The morning dawned all bright and sunshiny, and Marigold got up—and after dressing herself, put on the green shoes, and said, " I will wish for something lovely to-day."

She went downstairs and found her breakfast all ready. You see, yesterday's wish being gone, her father and mother had quite forgotten that she had wished for them not to worry about her. As soon as her breakfast was finished she ran outside, and said to herself, "I want to have a golden palace in the middle of Tanglewood."

A Golden Palace

Of course, she had quite forgotten to wish to be there at the same time. She was so excited, though, that the walk seemed quite easy. When she got exactly to the middle, there sure enough was an enormous golden palace, all made out of quite solid gold. She ran eagerly up to it and tried all the doors, but of course they wouldn't open because she had forgotten to wish for the key to let her into it. She walked wearily home and said, "To-morrow I will wish for a key."

The next day she *did* wish for a key, and finding it in her hand, she walked triumphantly to her palace again. The golden doors slid back easily at the touch of the key, and with a beating heart she stepped inside. To her horror and amazement, she found she had forgotten again, and there wasn't a bit of furniture in any of the rooms. So again she made her way desolately homewards, and said, "To-morrow I will be wiser, and will wish for everything I want at once."

So the next day she went out, and very quickly she said, "I want furniture for my palace, and servants, and a coach-and-four."

When she got there she found all these things waiting for her, but the furniture was so very grand that she dared not sit down on any of the chairs, and the servants, seeing that she did not understand,

And the Key.

More Wishes.

seemed to laugh at her. The four big black horses that were attached to her coach frightened her out of her wits as they kicked and reared; and, worst of all, she had forgotten to wish for her father and mother to be there too.

Now a terrible thing happened. She was so angry, this poor little Marigold, that she kicked off the green shoes and flung them into a corner of the state drawing-room, and a maid-servant, seeing them there, thinking they were old and not wanted, took them straight away and flung them into a corner of the palace courtyard. The maid was a forgetful person, and when Marigold came to look for the shoes the next morning they were nowhere to be found.

No
more
Wishes.

Somehow or another, she couldn't leave the magic palace, because, you see, she hadn't a "wish" to leave it; so for ten long years she had to live all alone with the servants that laughed at her, chairs she dared not sit on, and the horses that frightened her.

Now it happened one day that she was walking in the courtyard, very lonely, and looking very beautiful, and she said to herself, " Oh, how I wish I could have the green shoes back for a minute—for it is an awful thing to be shut up in this terrible place, and to know that everybody is getting old and grey looking for me."

And just at this minute she spied the shoes lying in the corner of the courtyard where they had been for years. She ran quickly to them, and casting off her own golden shoes, put on the shabby old green ones. She then wished very hurriedly, " Please send me my fairy prince to rescue me, like they do in all the fairy stories, and make father and mother and the little old woman as young as they were when I left them."

And all of a sudden before her stood, not clad in golden armour a prince, but the miller's son, whom she had known as a curly-headed little boy—grown up now, stalwart and handsome, with his merry

Another
Chance.

18

blue eyes shining, and his graceful sun-tanned neck gleaming through the low collar of his spotless white shirt. She looked at him very doubtfully.

"You are not a prince," she said; and he held out his arms.

Her Prince.

"I am *your* prince," he answered. "I have a head to think for you, hands to work for you, and a heart to love you with." And suddenly she found herself in his arms.

"I will take you home," he said; and hand in hand they went out into Tangle-wood, which was all one maze of sunshine.

When they got to the borders they passed the little old woman, who looked exactly the same, and she was so busy spinning that she did not notice them. On their way to Marigold's home they passed a little cottage covered with roses and eglantine, and from the little garden in front the breezes wafted to them the scent of sweetbriar.

"That is ours," said the miller's son,

pointing to the cottage; and Marigold said, "How beautiful!" and looked up at her prince. She had never said "How beautiful!" about the golden palace.

When she got home father and mother were just the same: no older, and looking at her with eyes full of longing. Of course they were surprised, for from being a little child she had grown into a tall and winsome maiden; but they loved her and kissed her in spite of all her faults, as all fathers and mothers do, or should do. And so it came to pass that one fine summer's day the marriage bells rang merrily, and Marigold and her prince were wedded.

Just after the marriage ceremony was over, Marigold suddenly said, "Oh, I forgot! I have the little old woman to see, and I must go alone."

So she went to the borders of Tanglewood, and found the little old woman spinning.

"I have brought you your shoes back,"

she said, holding them out in her hand,
" and I have got everything I wish : the
most beautiful cottage and the handsomest prince in the world."

"But you had the golden palaces,"
said the little old woman.

"Yes," said Marigold, "but they were
cold and lonely."

Work brings happiness. "You see I was right," said the little
old woman, and with a small, queer smile,
the green shoes once more on her feet,
she went on spinning flax.

EFFIE H. FREEMANTLE.